What
Echo Heard

What Echo Heard

by

GORDON SOMBROWSKI

OOLICHAN BOOKS
FERNIE, BRITISH COLUMBIA, CANADA
2011

Library and Archives Canada Cataloguing in Publication

Sombrowski, Gordon, 1959-
    What echo heard / Gordon Sombrowski.

Short stories.
ISBN 978-0-88982-283-2 (bound).--ISBN 978-0-88982-279-5 (pbk.)

    I. Title.

PS8637.O4475W43 2011   C813'.6   C2011-905738-7

We gratefully acknowledge the financial support of the Canada Council for
the Arts, the British Columbia Arts Council through the BC Ministry of
Tourism, Culture, and the Arts, and the Government of Canada through
the Canada Book Fund, for our publishing activities.

Published by
Oolichan Books
P.O. Box 2278
Fernie, British Columbia
Canada V0B 1M0

www.oolichan.com

Cover design by David Drummond - www. salamanderhill.com
Cover photo by Henry Georgi - www.henrygeorgi.com

Printed in Canada

MIX
Paper from
responsible sources
FSC
www.fsc.org   FSC® C013916

To my family and to Fernie

CONTENTS

FOREWARD

Echo, a nymph of the mountains loves the sound of her own voice. But she is cursed for she can only foolishly repeat the words of others. Thus she is my muse.

There are a few people who are named and appear in the background of these stories as though they are there in their own character; this is because they, like the buildings and mountains, are a part of the landscape of Fernie. All the principal characters are creations of artifice.

THE RIDE

Bobby's dad was a hard drinking man who ran a logging truck that hauled logs for the small-time mill operators around the valley. Every Saturday Bobby's dad would get into his pickup truck and he'd make the rounds of the mill operators to collect his pay and to find new jobs. Some Saturdays, when his old man was feeling particularly ornery, he'd make Bobby join him for the rounds. After breakfast they'd drive out to see Henry Fyfe. He was a big operator who'd hand out the odd jobs to the small jobbers like Bobby's dad if he had extra work. It paid better than the small outfits did and Henry liked a better quality whiskey.

So Bobby would sit in the truck while his dad sat in the office with Henry and they'd shoot the shit. They'd drink Canadian Club until the jobs were sorted out. If there was little work there'd only be a shot or so, if there was more haggling to do then they might polish off a half a' bottle. Then Bobby's dad would get into the pickup and they'd drive on to Kubernik's.

Usually Kubernik would only have a few little jobs, but he stilled the best booze in the valley, or so Bobby's dad would say. "That Polak is cheaper than his brew, but man can he make a mean schnapps!" After that they'd hit a few of the other operators who needed a truck, and Bobby's old man would have a drink or two with each of them. How he'd remember the jobs Bobby couldn't say. He figured the old man might have had a notebook, although he wasn't much of a writer. When the old man got too unsteady to drive he'd put Bobby behind the wheel. Bobby learned to drive by the time he was eleven. He could barely touch the gas pedal and the clutch, and if he stalled the truck the old man'd hit him and holler, "You no good for nothin', you're never gonna make a trucker."

But Bobby had one experience in those days that was fun like nothing he ever did before or after. Sometimes when Bobby didn't need to be in school or his father was working a Saturday the old man would say, "C'mon Bobby I'm gonna show you how to be a trucker." And they'd leave early in the morning and head up into the bush, and then Bobby'd help his old man as best he could.

When seen from the valley, the logging and mining roads that ran along the slopes of the Rockies looked like they had been cut along a line drawn with a ruler, so straight was the tattoo they left on the mountainside. The roads were more like animal tracks only wider, muddier and with more ruts. Those logging roads were cut as steep as a "bucket of rust held together by string and wire" could take them. The ride up was made in the lowest gear, grinding against the gravel, muck and dirt; the ride down was a battle between brakes and heaven. It took a lot of guts and grit, and the grinding of teeth depending upon the disposition of the driver; and it took a capricious belief in gravity — there to get you down but not to stop you.

The bush roads were emptier in those days. There were no city and country slickers in expensive gear, hiking, mountain biking or moving about on garish contrivances with lots of chrome and big wheels and making a loud noise. There'd be the odd family, mostly poor, out picking berries; the hunter in season, usually on foot or horse, sometimes in an old pickup, but you could go a day or two and, if you went deep enough, weeks without seeing another person. Except of course where the logging was in full tilt. There the trucks would haul up and down as long as there was enough light to see, and even when there wasn't.

It was a cold clear morning just after spring break-up was ended. Bobby's dad was back behind the wheel of his truck working long days. The break-up was bad for making the loan payments and had been longer than it should have been. Bobby's dad roused him with a shake and growl. "Git up lazy bones, you can come help pay for your grub today." The old man had been drinking heavily the night before and his voice skidded like truck tires when you hit the brakes on a bush road. Bobby knew if he didn't get out of bed without complaint there'd be trouble. So he jumped into his clothes and ran into the kitchen. His mom handed him some toasted white bread with fried bacon on it, and a bag with his lunch and a thermos of coffee and said, "Now run along, don't make him wait. He's nasty today." And she rubbed her hip where her husband had pushed her into the cupboard because his morning coffee wasn't ready. But then she was hung-over too and her hands hadn't been steady enough to get the grinds into the basket, and she'd spilled, and it had all taken a little longer that morning.

Bobby mumbled through the bacon and bread in his

mouth, "Thanks Mom," and ran out the kitchen door and into the street where his old man was warming up the truck. He hopped in beside his dad. The cracked vinyl seat was cold and he wished he'd put on a heavier jacket. They sat in the truck in silence, Bobby knowing it was best to say nothing, and so nothing was said, until half way up the mountain on their first run the truck got stuck. Bobby didn't know if it was because his dad was jerking the wheel that day or if it was because he really couldn't avoid the deep rut, but they got stuck. The old man's ruddy face took on the hue of a purple bruise. The curses came like a mantra. His timbre a gnarl. "Damn it boy, git out there and pull the winch cable 'round that tree up there, we'll winch'er out."

Bobby undid the cable, his fingers going numb on the dirty, rusty, cold steel. He pulled on the cable as the winch unreeled. He hoisted the grapple hook and the steel wire over his shoulder as it came off the spool. The weight of the cable ground into his back as he pulled the length that unwound behind him. He changed the cable from shoulder to shoulder as he walked up the road to the tree his dad had bent a dirty finger toward. He pulled the cable around the tree, and secured the hook onto the cable so that when it tightened the hook would grapple the cable. His old man started the winch and slowly the truck came out of the mud bog. When they were clear of the deep ruts and the rig could make its own way Bobby had to unhitch the winch cable. To save time, rather than spool up the cable, Bobby wrapped the cable from end to end around the bumper of the truck and they continued on.

"Well that's a load lost." His father's voice was calmer than it had been. "We'll have to make it up."

Bobby looked at his father, his eyes seeking telltale signs. He was sure of it, the new calm lilt in his old man's voice usually gave it away. His father had taken a drink while they had been winching. Bobby sniffed, trying to smell whiskey. His eyes carefully snooped around looking for a bottle or a brown paper bag, though his old man had a hip flask with him at all times. "Just in case," as he liked to say. Bobby knew that a bottle was more dangerous than the flask which held less than a Mickey. A twenty-sixer would spell real trouble. But the old man usually didn't drink when he was hauling.

The early summer forest seduced the wanderer with trills of birds that had learned southern melodies and larches shimmering with fresh green and pines smelling of virginal promise above brooks that chuckled of the pleasures of supping from their pools. It was hard to resist the enchantment. Bobby, like many in the valley, was a swain of the mountains and never tired of them. But he could not see the charms that morning, not when the old man was in the state he was. The loading went slowly. His old man cursed and drove fast down the mountain. The unloading went slower yet. It was as though the mill workers knew his father was behind schedule. The old man drove back up into the bush ever faster. They got lucky, they didn't get stuck again.

By late afternoon, the light sweet stench of booze sweat hovered around his old man, who didn't get out of the truck any more. Bobby ran around checking the load. He heard his father yell at the loader operator when he questioned him about it. "What's the boy good for, if he can't check the load? You gotta train 'em when they're young, otherwise they ain't no good later on." The loader laughed. Bobby's dad yelled, "You're a cynical bastard!" But the loader knew the old man and his moods, and he liked baiting the drivers so he said, "You figure a boy can do the job of a man?"

"I don't figure it," Bobby's dad snapped back, "I know it. I did it when I was a young'un and I trained my boy. I'll bet you he's checked the load so good that he'll ride down the mountain on top."

The loader's eyebrows rose. He liked Bobby. "Now don't be stupid. Puttin' a boy up there to ride on the load."

Calling the old man stupid was like waving a red flag at a bull. Bobby looked up at the load nervously. His eyes darted from chain to chain that held the logs in place.

"C'mon now, that don't make sense, puttin' the boy's life at risk like that," the operator said, not because he was wise but rather because it was his habit to avoid culpability.

Bobby's father said, "Bullshit on you. The boy knows what he's doin', he can ride the load. I'll bet ya a bottle a' Crown Royal that he rides it all the way to the bottom."

"Shit man that's too dangerous!"

"What, you afraid you're gonna lose a bottle a'Crown!" His father spat the taunt.

"Fine, suit yourself," said the loader operator, "but I figure the boy deserves the bottle if he rides it to the bottom, not you."

"You're on," laughed his father.

Then looking at Bobby he hollered, "Git up there boy!"

Bobby knew by the mad dog, booze-glazed look in his father's eyes that he dare not contradict him. He pulled himself up onto the front tires of the trailer and from there, hanging on to the logs and the trailer bars that held the logs in place, he reached the top of the load. He sat on the topmost log, spreading his legs and pinning his feet against the logs around him. He gripped the heavy link chain with his shaking hands.

His father put the truck in gear and the rig roared, diesel belched, the dark clouds of exhaust swirled past the boy. Bobby looked like a small angel riding Beelzebub, his face streaked black from dirt and the tears of fear that had come as he climbed the logs. His blue eyes brilliant with awe, the muscles of his arms and shoulders strained as he hung on to the top log. A flying trail of dust, bark and branches followed in his wake. In the adrenalin fueled exhilaration of the first burst of speed he began to laugh and shout; but not with joy. Soon the rig was careening down the mountain; the trees on either side brushed past. Bobby ducked his head afraid he might be hit by any stray long branches of pine arching across the road. Instinct made him grip the chain more tightly each time the rig came too close to a tree. His eyes would shut tight and he bit his lower lip so hard that it began to bleed.

They sped down the mountain, the rig eased into a rhythm, groaning each time they entered a curve. The logs swayed with the trailer and held. Bobby thought that his old man must still be sober enough to control the truck. He comforted himself with the thought that the old man had never spilled a load yet and he'd surely had more to drink before. Bobby settled in as best he could on top of the logs.

His terror began to change, not so much subsiding, it took on a fatalistic hue. It would be wrong to say that a sense of calm settled over him. His mood was more akin to acceptance. If he survived he wanted to remember the moment as being joyful though the words he used were "a hoot".

The wind in his ears made a music that sounded like a chorus of angel wings fluttering beside him, and he thought they must be, for he could not hear the noise of the screaming belly of the diesel engine, nor the growl of the tires clutching the road. High up on the back of the beast of the load he could see the clear blue sky, and where the trees were not too high his shivering frame was lit by the sun.

His hands did not waver from the chain. They held

firm, two more links welded on. His legs clenched the log so tightly that he could feel the sharp edges of the bark's brown teeth biting into his skin through his jeans. The diesel fumes gave way to forest air that rushed into his nostrils, a medley of scents: pine and cedar, rot, dirt, turpentine and the sweat of sage and lavender that reminded him of his grandmother. When he looked to the right or left he saw a blur of light and shadow, and greens in blushes of emerald, grass, hunter and black, grey and brown. When he looked ahead the variegations came into focus and he saw towering trees on their ascent of the mountain, and he saw the cut of the dirt road, certain until the next curve.

The beast bawled and bellowed as it made its way down the track, its frame agitated, seeking to numb the boy with vibration, but Bobby held tight. They passed a trucker in a bigger more modern outfit on his way back up for his next load. The driver geared down to a crawl. Bobby's father didn't slow down. Bobby looked down at the driver whose eyes for a moment glared at his father and then opened in surprise when they recognized the frame of the boy at the top of the load. In an instant their rigs had passed and for a moment Bobby was choking in the dust raised by the other trucker.

The ride went on and Bobby, though no less fearful, became more confident that he would make it to the bottom. The pitch of the road became less steep as they reached the lower slopes of the mountain. The ditches opened up pushing the trees further away from the rig and Bobby felt the sun warm his back. For moments, when the load seemed steady, he thought he couldn't wait to brag to his friends about how he had ridden down the mountain and a lick of bravado made him almost feel he wouldn't be afraid of anything again.

Bobby said that the ride down seemed to take a long, long time while it was happening; but now in his memory it went more quickly than anything else he ever did. They got to the bottom of the mountain, and his old man pulled up on the side of the road, slowing the rig to a stop. Bobby eased from the log his body clutched. His hands were cut and bleeding from the hard edges of the chain, his arms and legs quivering as he stretched them. He saw that his father had gotten out of the truck and was looking up at him. The old man's mouth hung as though he were pulling it up from the ground to lift his eyes to stare at Bobby.

Bobby could see fear in the first glance, perhaps the fear the old man had that he might not find his boy on the top of the load. Then he saw what he thought might be the gleam of ridiculous pride. The old man hollered, "Git on down from there boy!" Bobby heard a hoot and the cackle of a laugh that seemed to tear from his father's frame. "Whooee, you done it boy!"

Bobby began very slowly and carefully to climb down, the muscles of his legs stuttering as they settled against the logs, his fingers slipping as they burned against the dirt and bark. He landed on the ground on his butt. The old man pulled him up, clapped him hard on the back, and said, "You're gonna be a man yet boy!" Then his father reached inside the truck and pulled out an object of brown paper that was wrinkled and pressed into the shape of a bottle, the neck of which was poking out from the stained wet edges of the bag. His father unscrewed the cap, passed the bottle to Bobby, and said, "Here boy, take a pull, you earned it." And Bobby did, he drank deeply, and though the whiskey burned on the way down, he did not stop. He gulped it down determined to drink to the bottom of the bottle. The old man wasn't going to get anymore out of that bottle. As he drank he swore to himself he'd never drink and he swore that he'd never be a trucker.

Bobby didn't keep the oaths he made that day. He never was a real trucker, "just to spite the old man" he'd said, though he admitted that "he'd done grocery delivery for Trites's once he got his licence." Sometimes he'd take a drink, and once for a while hit the bottle hard, but never whiskey. Mostly now he drinks coffee when he goes to the bar. Bobby likes going to bars and must have a soft spot for the drinking man because when he finished his story he said, "The old man took that bottle of Crown Royal I won, but I had one drink out of it with him, before he finished it off. The old man drank 'til the day he died. He wasn't a bad man, he just liked the booze."

MITTENS

"It won't be too bad. The sun shines here, too!" were the first words Zarah heard Mutti say about Fernie. Zarah, her mother Mutti, and Vati, her new father, the one Mutti married because Zarah's Papa had been felled by a bullet as he stood next to a birch tree somewhere in vast Russia, arrived in Fernie during the late hot days of July, when the waters of the Elk River began to meander among the rock beds tickling the feet of children bathing to cool themselves.

"Don't worry winter will come soon enough!" Vati said. And all three of them felt chilled. They had heard that the winters in Canada were hard, as hard as in Siberia, a place Vati had survived, a place he had told Zarah was Satan's creation of ice on earth.

But the summer was long and warm and then came what the people of the town called, "Indian Summer" and Zarah forgot about winter. Every day as she did her chores she imagined, reddish brown men named Winnetou who carried bows and arrows and women called Nscho-tschi with papooses climbing the mountains that she saw outside the windows of their apartment. She had never seen mountains before, and she marveled that something could go so high into the air. She felt sure the mountains must keep the sky from falling down. The mountains frightened her, but in the way a very old man, though he is kindly, frightens a child. Zarah liked it best when the morning sun shone on the peaks of the mountains for then they looked like they might be cathedrals, like the cathedral Zarah had seen in the big city near her old village.

It was during the days of Indian Summer that the first day of school arrived. On this day of her first year in Canada Zarah entered grade one. Zarah was afraid to go to school, though not because she did not like to learn. Mutti said, "My angel, do not be afraid of the Canadian school, you speak English, you are smart and you will learn." But Zarah was frightened because she knew that people made fun of the way she spoke English. The children she had tried to play with laughed at her. The pimply shop clerks laughed at her when she did the shopping for the family. Zarah was luckier than most immigrant children who came to Canada because her Mutti had worked for the English Occupation Forces and Zarah had learned a kind of English *patois* from the soldiers. A *patois* that included words like "bloody and blimey and blasted" which tickled the Fernie ear in a way a feather might.

Mutti walked Zarah to the school with its tall red brick pilasters and long rectangular windows. They went into the office and then after some moments a big woman in a dress of bright red, yellow and green flowers told Mutti and Zarah to follow her. They walked down the long hallway that led to the elementary classrooms. They entered a doorway and Zarah looked with big eyes. The woman and the teacher spoke, Mutti looked and listened carefully though she did not understand most of what they said, and then Mutti kissed Zarah on the cheek and in German said, "Darling Zarah, go sit at the desk there and when school is finished walk home. I will see you when I come home from work." The teacher frowned.

Zarah seated herself and looked about the classroom. On the black board she saw the alphabet printed in big white chalk letters. On the wall hung posters with letters of the alphabet and with a picture of a word that started with that letter, so that Zarah saw that "B" was for book and "C" was for cat.

The teacher clapped her hands and said, "Good Morning Children. Welcome to my class and to your first day of school. My name is Mrs. Smythe." The teacher, wore a pencil slim grey skirt, a sharply pressed white blouse and a black sweater and, with a turn as tight as her bun, she faced the black board and printed the letters "MRS. SMYTHE". Then she spun back and picked up a ruler from her desk and pointed at each letter and said the letter. She faced the class and looking from face to face said, "You will call me Mrs. Smythe, not teacher. And you will put up your hand when you wish to speak."

She picked up a sheet of paper from her desk and said, "Every morning I will call the roll. I will say your name and you will put up your hand and say 'Present.'" She started, "William Appleby", and a little boy giggled and put up his hand and said, "Present." Next the teacher said, "Mary Carnes" and so the teacher continued, and Zarah watched the tall lank woman who though not old seemed to have wrinkles and pinched lips and eyes hidden behind black cat's eye glasses.

The teacher said, "*Sara Shmid*". There was a pause and

silence. The teacher said the words "*Sara Shmid*" more loudly. The children stopped fidgeting in their desks. The teacher shouted, "*Sara Shmid*" and looked at Zarah. The children all looked at Zarah.

Zarah looked up at the teacher who stepped toward her desk. The teacher stopped short of the desk and took the ruler she had in the pocket of her skirt and pointed at Zarah and said, "You are *Sara Shmid*. Hand up and say 'Present.'" Zarah's face turned red and slowly she put her hand up and in a voice so small said, "Present."

The teacher's face changed, her lips writhing into a sneer, "So you're the little Nazi." The teacher turned and began to walk back to her desk.

Zarah burst out in English that was clear and clipped as though she had been born a Cockney in the East End of London and educated at Oxford, "I am no bloody Nazi. My name is Zarah Schmied." The teacher stopped. The children inhaled as one. The teacher turned back towards Zarah. The woman looked surprised as though astounded by the accent but the rancour in her eyes showed she was not prepared to tolerate any insolence. Her voice loud and merciless, she said, "You're a Kraut, and you're all the same."

The children laughed, the teacher shouted, "Silence!"

Mrs. Smythe took two steps towards Zarah, scowled at her and with bite said, "Hand out." Zarah looked up the length of the woman nervously and whispered, "I beg pardon."

"Put your hand out!"

Zarah did as she was told. She extended the palm of her hand and the teacher using the ruler hit Zarah on the hand so that it cracked throughout the room. The other little children's eyes opened in terror as Zarah's eyes squinted shut in pain. She willed herself not to cry out and she pressed her legs not to pee. And she did not. Her face went a deeper red and her eyes opened big and slowly a silent tear rolled out. The teacher turned away from Zarah and strode towards her desk where she picked up the list of names and called out the name, "Peter Small". And the little boy two desks behind Zarah whispered, "Present."

Zarah, Mutti and Vati lived in the Queen's Apartments on the third floor in a little one bedroom apartment. The apartment smelled of must, and deep pans of fried onions, and clothes drying, and twigs of pine and cedar that Mutti and Zarah had cut and placed in jars of water to freshen the air. The apartment was either too hot or too cold depending on the temperament of the steam boiler, but Mutti said, "We must not complain, we have a good roof over our head and one day soon we will have our own house."

Vati worked as a mechanic, the trade he had learned in Germany. He worked for a logging operation in the bush. Sometimes he would be in the bush for days at a time, and then he would come back, dirty and tired but he would unroll a wad of dollar bills and say, "Look how much money I have made. The others they drink it up, but we will save it so that we can buy a house." Mutti cooked and cleaned at the King Edward Hotel and when she came home from work at the hotel, she would find boiled peeled potatoes or fried potatoes and a bit of meat and boiled cabbage warming on the stove. Plates and forks and knives would be laid out on the table. She would say, "*Ach Zarahchen Du bist ein liebes Mädchen.*" Zarah who liked to practice translating her mother's words would repeat them softly in English, "Little Zarah you are a dear little girl."

The snow started to fall, as it often did in those days, at

Halloween. The little family did not know what Halloween was and did not dress Zarah in a costume and take her out to call for caramel apples and popcorn balls and goody bags. Though Zarah heard the other children talk about it, and Mrs. Smythe showed them how to make paper cut-out Jack o'lanterns, Zarah did not understand what they meant by Trick or Treat.

On Halloween night Zarah looked out the window of the apartment as children ran by the building in shapes of ghouls and ghosts. But she hardly saw them as she contemplated the wonder of the snow. For days the snow kept falling and every day Zarah looked out the windows of the apartment and watched the snowflakes descend, dancing like Salome, flake by flake, seducing the world into winter. Zarah looked at the piling white banks of snow and asked, worry in her voice, "Mutti, do you think the snow will come this high, do you think we'll be buried in snow."

Mutti would smile and say, "Isn't it good we live so high, the snow will never come this high." How surprised Mutti was when she saw that so much snow fell that the snow had to be shoveled up off the roofs of the coal miner's cottages. Laughing she said to Vati, "Ernst promise me we buy a two story house, I don't want to drown in the snow."

Vati said, "Don't worry Gretel we will buy a big house with a garden for Zarah to play in."

On the first day of December Zarah awoke and at breakfast her Mutti pointed at the wall where Zarah saw hung on the dingy grey wall paper a colourful poster board. Mutti said, "It is your Advent Calendar, my dear."

Zarah ran to the pretty Advent Calendar that was, but for the Fernie Quality Meat Market Calendar, the only ornament on the walls of the room. Zarah looked at the Advent Calendar with delight. Her mother helped her open the door with the number 1 on it. It became something they did each morning. Together with Mutti she would point her finger and trace the number of the day it was and then open the little cut-out door beneath the number to see what was hidden behind it. Each day there was another little surprise: an angel, a harp, a shepherd, his sheep, a star, a tree, a candle. Each was different and each was prettier than the one before.

Zarah did not notice that the calendar was hand-made. She adored looking at the images hidden by the doors. Zarah did not know that Mutti had gone from shop to shop in Fernie and asked, "Have you Advent Calendar?" And all of the shop keepers looked at her suspiciously and shook their heads. Some said they had never heard of such a thing. Others just looked at Mutti like she was not speaking English, which was perhaps not unfair so strong was Mutti's German accent. So Mutti sat down after Zarah was asleep and worked three whole nights and made the calendar with paper, scissors and glue, glitter and Christmas wrapping and the Eaton's catalogue.

Every day after opening the calendar, eating her breakfast and putting on her heavy grey woolen stockings, green loden coat, boots bought at Trites Wood, red mittens, red scarf and little red woolen cap, Zarah would walk to school. The townspeople would look at the blonde hair curling from under the cap and the blue eyes and some would think of Shirley Temple as Heidi. She walked past the shops on Main Street and she saw the shopkeepers and their clerks begin to decorate the windows with Christmas decorations. She admired the gold and silver paper garlands draped from the corner of the window frames. She saw boxes wrapped in green and red with ribbons and bows. She saw sleighs being ridden by teddy bears, train sets, and dolls with golden hair.

She knew this meant Christmas must be coming, but only the Advent Calendar made her feel that the arrival of Christmas was near.

In the first week of Advent came the day on the calendar marked 6. Behind that red and green door was a little man in a gold mitre and a red robe who held a long hooked cane. Mutti said, "Oh Zarah look, today comes St. Nikolaus." So that morning Zarah asked Mutti if she could put on her special ribbon for her hair, and she walked to school in nervous anticipation. Would St. Nikolaus give her a treat or would *Knecht Ruprecht* give her a lump of coal? She had asked Mutti at the door of the apartment as she put on her coat, "Mutti I have been a good girl haven't I?"

Mutti's eyes twinkled and she said, "*Zarahchen* you are the best little girl St. Nikolaus will find today."

Life in school had taken on an order that Zarah did not understand or question. Each morning Mrs. Smythe would say, "Good Morning Class." All the children would say, "Good Morning Mrs. Smythe." And then the roll call would begin and when Zarah heard the words, "*Sara Shmid*" she put up her hand and said, "Present." The rest of each day passed in peace, which is to say that Mrs. Smythe did not call on Zarah. It was as though Zarah was not in the classroom. Zarah pulled out her books when the other children pulled out their books and she quietly read what the other children read aloud and she coloured and she printed and she sat in school all day long and she learned the things a first grader was supposed to learn. But never once did Mrs. Smythe speak to her. And Zarah, either because she was stubborn or she was afraid or she was shy, did not speak to Mrs. Smythe. She never asked to be excused to go to the toilet. She held it until the bell for the break rang and then, as the children ran out of the classroom she ran to the toilet. Once she had finished she would stay in the toilet stall until the warning bell rang and then she would go back to the classroom. At lunch she ran home as fast as she could and then she would eat some of the sticky white bread and hard yellow cheese it seemed people in Canada ate. Then she would run back to school just as the bell rang.

On that first Nikolaus day in Canada, like every day, the clock at the front of the classroom showed the hours slowly go by, but on this day, a day on which Zarah hoped for the arrival of St. Nikolaus, the clock moved especially slowly. If the classroom door opened Zarah expected to see St. Nikolaus, but he did not come and when the minute hand began to reach for the number 3 she knew that neither St. Nikolaus nor even *Knecht Ruprecht* would appear.

The end of day bell rang and all the children laughed and shouted and left the school. Zarah walked home wondering where St. Nikolaus had been. "Maybe," she said as she trudged her boots through the snow, "he can't get to Fernie because there is too much snow."

In the dimming light of the winter day she fried the potatoes and laid out the plates and waited for her Mutti and Vati to come home. She looked out the window and hoped and hoped and hoped that St. Nikolaus would find Fernie, but the streets emptied and the town was dark but for the light of houses that penetrated the snow that hadn't stopped falling all day. When her Mutti came in the door, she ran to her and said, "Mutti, Mutti, St. Nikolaus didn't come."

Mutti said, "What do you mean, he didn't come."

"He didn't come to school. I don't think he can find Fernie."

Mutti hugged her and said, "My child, my child, surely St. Nikolaus will find Fernie, it might take him a bit longer, but he will come."

All that evening Zarah waited for a knock on the door to announce the arrival of St. Nikolaus, but no knock came. She looked at her mother with a sad face, but Mutti just smiled and said, "Zarah put out your stockings on the bed post. When St. Nikolaus comes he'll find them." Zarah hung her stocking wondering if she would find treats or a lump of coal left by *Knecht Ruprecht* or anything at all. Zarah said to her Mutti, "I'll wait up until he comes then I can ask him if it was hard to get through the snow to come to Fernie." And so she lay in bed staring out the window listening for the sound of steps on the stairs until she fell asleep.

As soon as Zarah was in bed and the door to the bedroom closed Mutti said to Vati, "Ernst I must go out to find something for Nikolaus."

"Oh don't be silly, she can do without Nikolaus; there is no Nikolaus in this country. The men at work told me."

"There is for our Zarah."

Vati just sighed. It was hard to get used to this new land.

Mutti put on her boots and coat and hat and with determination she walked through the snowy streets to Mrs. Abry's sweet shop. The little shop was in the house in the block next to the school, and the children who had money would go to Abry's to buy candies each day. Mr. and Mrs. Abry lived upstairs in the house and so Mutti knocked on their door. Luckily Mrs. Abry answered the door, and even more luckily Mrs. Abry spoke German, for she had emigrated from a German speaking land too, but before the First Great War.

Mutti said, "Dear Mrs. Abry, today is *Nikolaustag* and my little Zarah said no Nikolaus came to the school."

Mrs. Abry, was a soft round plump woman, and had a sharpness to her laugher, though she was kind. She thought some of the newly arrived immigrants didn't pay enough attention. She said, "Frau Schmied, there is no *Nikolaustag* in Canada."

Mutti, looked despondent, "I know. My husband told me this. But it is too late, I can't tell Zarah there is not *Nikolaustag*. Nikolaus must come tonight, can you not sell me some sweets."

Mrs. Abry was always anxious to make a sale. There was a mortgage to pay and her own children to feed and clothe. They went into the shop and Mrs. Abry turned on the light above the candy counter. Mutti did not know the candies. They looked different than the sweets in Germany. She said, "*Ach* Mrs. Abry, so many lovely candies, which ones might a little girl like."

"How much would you like to spend?" asked Mrs. Abry.

"I have fifty cents." Mutti said proudly.

Mrs. Abry had hoped Mutti would say a dollar, but fifty cents was better than nothing and so she packed up the candies and threw in a couple of extras since, as she said to Mutti, "I am an immigrant too, we have to help each other!"

The next morning, as Zarah pulled from her stocking red, green, pink and blue candies and a lollipop and foil wrapped chocolates, she told her mother that she had heard St. Nikolaus come into her room and behind him stood *Knecht Ruprecht* smiling at her with a sinister turn to his lips. Zarah said she asked, "Did you have trouble getting through the snow?"

She said he whispered in her ear, "My child the crows led me through the snow to find you." From that day Zarah loved the crows and she would talk to them whenever she saw them.

After laying out all the candies in a row on her little dresser she went to school. Though she did not speak with many of the children, or rather many of the children did not speak with her, there was a boy who spoke with her every now and then. This boy came from the rough part of town next to the train tracks in the North End. He liked her blond hair and blue eyes more than he feared her because she was the enemy.

Zarah asked him, "What did St. Nikolaus bring you?" He frowned, "Who is St. Nikolaus?" Then he laughed in a funny way, which wasn't quite mean but which she knew meant that he thought she was strange. Then he said, "Santa Claus doesn't come until Christmas." And he pulled her braid, and ran to sit down as Mrs. Smythe called the class to order.

It grew colder and the big school house windows were always fogged or frozen over and the steam registers spit and sputtered and hissed in a way that reminded Zarah of her cat "Mausi" that she had had to leave behind in the village in Germany. Her classmates began to chatter ever more of Santa Claus, and they cut out paper to make snowflakes, and they made garlands of red and green, and the teacher read them a poem, "Twas the night before Christmas." Zarah went home to Mutti and asked, "Mutti will Santa Claus come to us?"

Mutti looked at Zarah with eyes that betrayed surprise. "What is that you ask my child?"

"Santa Claus, will Santa Claus come to visit us?"

Mutti didn't know what to say. She had heard something about this Santa Claus man. She had seen pictures of a fat, white-bearded man in a red suit. In the King Edward Hotel the bartenders decorated the bar with a life size cardboard cutout of him holding a Coca Cola bottle. Mutti looked at him skeptically each day as she cleaned the bar, surprised that such a man meant for children should be in a place where men drank and smoked. As she scrubbed the floor around the figure she wanted to push it over, make him go away. He was not a part of Christmas for Mutti. "You are an imposter," she muttered at the cardboard. Yet every night at home as they washed the dishes Zarah asked, "Mutti will Santa Claus visit us like the children in school say?"

Zarah walked past the houses on her way to and from school and looking in the windows she saw Christmas trees go up in the sitting rooms. Yet no Christmas tree went up in the apartment. She asked her mother, "Mutti, why do we not have a Christmas tree?" To which her mother said, "My darling, all things come to those who are patient." And Zarah would sigh and go to bed a little more worried each night that there was no tree in their apartment when in all the windows of the houses of the town there was a tree to see.

Then something happened that gave Zarah comfort. Not too many days before the Christmas break, Mrs. Smythe said to the class, "Children, this afternoon we are going to make an ornament for your Christmas tree. The tradition of the Christmas Tree comes from Germany." And then for the first time since the day she had hit Zarah she addressed the child, "It's one of the few good things that has. Sara do you have a Christmas tree?"

Zarah shook her head, her eyes tearing so that she could not look at Miss Smythe and she looked down at her lap. "Silly girl," said the teacher shrugging her shoulders, "You're a kraut, you must." The class laughed.

Zarah worked hard to make the little drum that the teacher showed them how to fashion from two circles of cardboard and a piece of paper they coloured and then glued together and trimmed with red ribbon to make the hanger. As she cut the paper Zarah's face stopped burning for she had a happy thought, "I'm from Germany where the Christmas tree comes from." And she repeated it to herself "I'm from Germany where the Christmas tree comes from." And then she wanted to shout, "I'm from Germany where the Christmas tree comes from" for she knew that if St. Nikolaus could find her all the way from Germany than surely she, too, would have a Christmas tree. But she pressed her lips together in a smile and cut her paper quietly. Mrs. Smythe thought it unfair that a little German child could look so angelic.

The last day of school before the holidays came and Mrs. Smythe wished the whole class a Merry Christmas and the class shouted back, "Merry Christmas Mrs. Smythe!" and Zarah did too. Then came the morning when Zarah opened the little door in the calendar with the number 24 on it. Inside was a picture of a miniature evergreen tree with a gold star on the top of it. But still there was no tree in the apartment. As Mutti made the porridge for breakfast she said to her daughter, "Vati and I have to work today. Zarah, my child, tonight the Christ child will visit us and we must make sure the apartment is as clean and pretty as possible." So Zarah shook out the curtains, wiped the window sills, dusted the chairs, swept and washed the floors, made the beds. When she thought the house was clean enough even for the Christ child she pulled her little trunk from under her bed and carefully removed the box she had decorated to hold the little paper drum that she had made. She placed it on the sill of the window next to the Advent Calendar. As the daylight grew dim she peeled the potatoes for dinner, then she sat down and looked out the window across the white roofs of the town to the black trees on the edges of the mountains. The pines, spruces and cedars laden with an ermine shawl of white looked warm against the grey cloud that hid the mountains. As she looked she fell asleep and dreamed of her Omi in Germany and her cat Mausi and her friends in the village.

Zarah awoke to the bang of the door as her mother rushed in. It looked like she might be carrying a package. Her mother bustled through the room and into the bedroom where she and her parents slept. "Zarah, *schnell*, we must get dressed for church. I had to work late today and now we must hurry to go to church." Zarah quickly changed out of her house dress and into her best dress, a beautiful dress that her Omi had made and sent to her from Germany for Christmas. Zarah didn't recognize the purple velvet and lace but Mutti did and knew that her mother had cut up her own going to church dress. Zarah's mother rushed about as she changed and soon the two were dressed and were out the door and on their way to the Anglican Church.

Zarah and her mother and stepfather were Lutherans but there was no Lutheran Church in Fernie and so they went to the Anglican Church, though no one knew them.

As they walked to the church, Zarah suddenly realized that her stepfather was not with them, "Mutti where is Vati? Shouldn't he be going to church with us?"

"Oh, my child, he had to work late, he will come to join us if he can."

"But why does he have to work late, it's Christmas?"

Zarah's mother, though she sighed, smiled, "People still work on Christmas Eve in Canada, it is different than at home," she corrected herself, "than in Germany. See even I had to work late today, but my dear tomorrow we both shall not work and we shall all have a lovely day together."

And then they went into the church and listened to the words of Canadian Christmas which, though they did not fully understand, told a story they knew. Zarah saw Mrs. Smythe across the congregation, but Mrs. Smythe did not see her.

The choir sang "Hark the Herald Angels Sing" and

"Angels We Have Heard on High" and then "Silent Night". Zarah's Mutti hummed to herself and she squeezed Zarah's hand so that it hurt, and Zarah looked up at her mother and tried to wriggle her hand free of her mother's grip.

After the service was over they made their way with the crowd towards the door of the church. Zarah and her Mutti stayed far to the edge of the parishioners who were all exchanging Christmas greetings and, though no one spoke to them, Zarah saw a few kind smiles. They walked out of the church into the cold night air. Mutti tried to sidle past the Vicar when he stepped through the people in front of them and shook Mutti's hand and then shook Zarah's hand and in a loud voice so that all the other people could hear it he said, "Merry Christmas to you." And Zarah saw her Mutti blush red and they both said, "Merry Christmas!" and though no one else said anything to them, Zarah felt something important had happened, though she did not know what it was.

Then Zarah's Mutti said, "Let us go home, maybe your Vati will be home then, too." They walked down the street, past the Catholic Church, and Zarah's Mutti said, "Aren't the windows pretty, look at the colours. It is like our church at home." And they walked on, Zarah holding her mother's hand as they crossed the street and stopped in front of the Court House which loomed a dark silhouette against the night sky of moon-glossed clouds. Zarah shivered. Her Mutti felt the tremble through her gloves. "Are you cold my little one?"

"No," said Zarah.

"What then?"

"It is such a scary building," said Zarah.

Her Mutti laughed, "Don't be frightened of this place. This is a good place. Here lives justice."

"Mutti, what is the statue?" and she pointed her red mittened hand to the sculpture in the courtyard of the building.

"My dear, that is a cenotaph, that is where they put the names of all the soldiers who died in the war. Your papa is on a stone just like that in the village at home."

Then Zarah noticed a figure moving in the courtyard before the judicial edifice. The dark shadow of a long over-coat dragged in the deep snow. A woman was walking toward the base of the tall statue of the beautiful young soldier. His head was bent in mourning, his hand hold-ing a cross set in the stone poppies of Flanders. The wom-an walked as quickly as the mounds of snow around the Cenotaph would let her. Zarah let go of her Mutti's hand and tracing the foot prints leading to the Cenotaph she walked towards the statue. Her Mutti said, "Zarah what are you doing? Come back." But Zarah did not stop. She walked toward the foot of the statue, and stood in the black shadow of the woman.

In the dark night the glow of the moon played from cloud to cloud and Zarah could see the white snow that rested on the stone soldier's grey hat and shoulders but his face was dark and she could not see his expression. Then she looked down to the base of the statue and there she saw a single red rose the woman had placed there. The woman did not move and Zarah took a step to stand beside her. Zarah looked up at the woman's face and she started. It was Mrs. Smythe, and she saw that Mrs. Smythe was crying. Looking at the base of the statue she saw that there were names and she saw black letters set into the stone.

Mutti called, "Zarah, what are you doing? Don't be silly come, we must go." But Zarah looked at the dark letters of the names against the grey granite. She spelled the names she saw saying each letter until she began to spell the letters "S", "M","Y", "T", "H", "E" and she saw that the name was "James Smythe".

Zarah lifted her red mittened hand and grasped the black gloved hand of Mrs. Smythe. Mrs. Smythe startled, realizing for the first time that the child was there. Zarah held the woman's hand tightly and said, "My papa is dead too."

Mrs. Smythe looked down at the child, her eyes wet, uncomprehending, and then she said, "Oh." The two stood in silence.

Mutti called again, "Zarah come, come we must go home. Vati will be home and wondering what has happened to us."

Mrs. Smythe looked down at Zarah and said, "You'd better run along." Zarah glanced at the name one more time and then retraced her steps and joined her mother, "That was my teacher Mrs. Smythe."

Mutti nodded with a frown.

As they walked back to the apartment heavier darker clouds began to blow over the edge of the Lizard Range. A black billow shrouded the light of the moon and snowflakes began to fall as they opened the door to the Queen's Apartment House. They climbed the creaky stairs and Mutti said loudly, "I hope Vati is home." Then she stamped her feet to shake off the snow and they shed their mittens, gloves, hats and just outside the door they took off their coats. Zarah's mother opened the door. The apartment was still and dark but for the glow of light that came from the corner of the room. Zarah's eyes opened wide, her lips parted in an "ooh". Next to the window was a spruce tree and on it burned candles and from each bough hung a different colourful glass ornament. Zarah did not move. She looked and was afraid to blink in case the beautiful tree disappeared. Mutti and Vati hugged her and kissed her and then each other and said, "*Frohe Weihnachten*".

Zarah asked, "Did Santa Claus come?" And Vati and Mutti looked at each other and Mutti said, "No Zarah, the Christ child came. He is the one who brings the light of the tree at Christmas."

Mutti saw how Zarah looked uncertain, so she asked, "What is it my dear?"

Zarah said, "In school the children said that Santa Claus is coming." Mutti smiled, "Don't worry my child, the Santa Claus he will come too."

"But when? All the children in school said he would come at Christmas."

Vati and Mutti, smiled as they looked at her. They, too, had learned about Santa Claus and so Vati said, "Don't be impatient Zarah. Santa Claus will come."

Mutti said, "Wait till tomorrow morning and you will see if the Santa Claus has come. Santa Claus only comes during the night when you are asleep."

They arranged the kitchen chairs next to the tree. The chrome frame and yellow vinyl seat and back of the chairs was made grotesque by the gentle glow of the candles. Zarah sat between Mutti and Vati, and they each held one of her hands. Mutti began to sing, "*Es ist ein Ros Entsprungen*". Her voice was thin and warbled so that she sounded like she was far away. Vati's voice, stronger, baritone, brought the soprano tones back into the room and the two sounded like an organ where only the big pipes and the littlest pipes worked. The final phrase of the song was not yet finished before Vati began to sing "*Oh Tannenbaum*" and now Zarah sang too. She knew the words of the ode to the tree and she sang them as loudly as she could because she wanted the

Christmas tree to know how happy she was. Then they sang "*Kling Glöckchen, Kling*". Last of all they sang "*Stille Nacht*" and Zarah tried to sing too, but the words that came out of her mouth were, "silent night, holy night" and Mutti sighed when she heard it until tears of her homesickness made her forget that too.

Vati wiped his eyes. Smiling at Zarah, he said, "Come *Zarahchen*, let us see what the Christ Child has brought you." Zarah jumped off her chair and kneeled in front of the tree. She could see that the big package had her name on it, but she did not know who the little packages were for. Vati kneeled beside her. He picked up the first package, shook it and said, "This one is for you Zarah from Mutti and me."

Zarah carefully opened the package. There was a little doll, with a round head and painted curly blond hair and painted blue eyes, and a pretty pink dress. Zarah hugged Mutti and Vati and kissed them.

Then Vati said, "This package is for Mutti." And Zarah took the present from his hand and placed it in the hands of her mother. They all watched as Mutti unwrapped the package. It was towels, something which Mutti was thankful for.

"What about for you Vati, did the Christ Child bring a present for you?"

Vati smiled, "Yes, yes he did, here it is." And Vati unwrapped the present and it was a pair of work gloves which meant warmer hands for him.

"What about the big present?" Zarah asked excited, "It's for me isn't it?"

"Oh yes, the big box, I just about forgot. It is from the Christ Child." Vati laughed.

Zarah went to the parcel and began to pull at the paper. As she pulled away the paper she saw that it wasn't a parcel at all, it was a sleigh. A sleigh with wooden and red metal runners.

Zarah laughed and shouted and said, "We must go for a sleigh."

Mutti, said, "No, no Zarah it's too late at night, its dark. But tomorrow we will."

Then Zarah remembered that she had a present to give, so she went to the window sill and took down the little box. She brought it to Mutti and said, "I have a present for you and Vati." Mutti carefully unwrapped the package and there she saw the little paper drum. She kissed Zarah and said, "It's beautiful. Look Ernst, look what Zarah made." Then Mutti placed the little paper drum on the middlemost bough of the tree so that it could be seen from all sides of the room. Zarah felt a pleasure greater even than the joy of receiving a sleigh, and she was happy like she could not remember being happy before.

Mutti made hot chocolate and they sat and ate the Christmas cookies and *Stollen* that Mutti and Zarah had baked the week before. Finally Mutti said, "Now it is bed time Zarah or Santa Claus will not come." Zarah was tired and though delighted with the gifts she had received thought she had better go to sleep to make sure Santa Claus came.

The next morning Mutti came into the room and opened the curtains and said, "Up, up my sleepy head." Zarah looked about the room, her eyes looking for a sign that Santa Claus had been there. Out the window the sky was already blue and from her bed she could see the first pink of the sun touching the white mountain tops.

"Mutti did Santa Claus come?"

"Out of bed look for yourself!" Mutti laughed.

Zarah jumped out of bed and ran into the main room. There, next to the Christmas tree was one of her stockings. It was oddly bulky. She ran to it and picking it up placed it on the kitchen table. She emptied it very slowly. It was filled with candies and a mandarin orange and there was a little colouring book. She looked at it, not so much with disappointment, as with uncertainty. She blurted out, "Mutti, the Christ child brought me better presents."

Mutti looked over at Zarah. Zarah noticed that just for an instant Mutti's eyes looked like someone had pinched her, then Mutti smiled, and said, "Zarah, you must be thankful for every gift you receive no matter how big or small or even unwelcome. The Santa Claus, like the Christ child, only comes to grateful children."

Zarah looked at her mother, and a tear of remorse rolled over her cheek. "I'm sorry Mutti. Sorry Santa Claus." Her voice so filled with shame that Mutti came to her and held her firmly against her bosom. Then Vati said, "What? Tears on Christmas morning! C'mon let's go for a sleigh ride."

"First breakfast Ernst!" laughed Mutti.

The first day of school after the holidays was clear and cold. The sun shone but there was no heat from its rays to warm the apartment and the windows of the apartment became translucent with thick frost. Vati said, "It is very, very cold. Zarah should not go to school."

Mutti only said, "We have a roof over our heads, we have heat and we have good food to eat. We'll just put more clothes on, it's not like in '46 when we had no shoes and gloves and nothing to eat. Zarah has to go to school or the people here will not think well of us."

Mutti gave Zarah long underwear to put on under her stockings and two undershirts, and she wrapped Zarah's face with an extra scarf and put a pair of her own mittens over Zarah's red mittens. And because it was so cold she walked with Zarah as far as the King Edward Hotel and Zarah stood in the back door of the kitchen and warmed up. She watched as Mutti took off her coat and hat and gloves and put on an apron and started to work washing the big stack of dishes that awaited her. The breakfast cook offered Zarah a biscuit she had baked that morning but Zarah shook her head and said, "No thank you." For her mother had told her to never take food if she came to the hotel kitchen.

When Zarah was warmed she continued walking the last two blocks to school.

The children playing outside ran and shouted as though it were a summer day. When they saw Zarah walking towards the school in her loden coat and her mother's scarf some of the older boys began to throw snowballs at her. The snow had frozen hard and the balls were sharp blocks of ice. One hit Zarah on the small of her back and she lost her balance and fell. The weight of all the clothes made it hard for her to lift herself from the ground but she rolled over and then struggled to her feet. The boys picked up more chunks of snow. The biggest of the boys lobbed a big lump that arced high and just missed Zarah's shoulder, landing on the frozen ground. It shattered and sprayed her stockings with crystals of snow that caught the sun so that her leggings looked like they had been embroidered with little splinters of glass. Zarah yelped and wanted to run, but she knew that was not the right thing to do. So she took a step and one more step towards the school door. Another snowball hit her on the back.

She heard, "You! Stop that right now!" She turned, the voice familiar, and though she did not trust it, it was the voice of adult authority. In the first moment of recognition she wondered if she were being singled out. There was Mrs. Smythe. The teacher pulled the arm of the biggest boy. A snow ball dropped from his hand. The other boys ran away. The biggest boy stood as Mrs. Smythe said something to him. Then Mrs. Smythe walked to Zarah and without saying a word she held out her black gloved hand. Zarah looked up at Mrs. Smythe. Then Zarah placed her hand into the teacher's and the two walked up the stairs and into the school.

MARIA ASSUNTA'S MIRACLES

1

Maria Assunta Belfiore saw the Blessed Virgin Mary. This was the first of her miracles. Anyone who looked in the window and saw her standing in front of her kitchen sink washing dishes would not have thought that she had experienced one miracle, let alone three. Looking through her perfectly cleaned panes they would see a woman with thick ankles and swollen feet stuffed into her pantofoles, as she called the fleece-lined felt slippers she dragged about the house. They would see a woman who had a dark mole, as dark and dull though not quite as big as her eyes, one inch above the right corner of her thin frowning lips. From the mole grew a hair which was black, as black as the hair on her head. Maria Assunta had a full round face which was little lined, as she was rather plump, so that her face and body were in harmony with her ankles.

Most people never saw Maria Assunta standing over her kitchen sink. If they saw her at all they would see Maria Assunta in her chocolate brown beret, thick cable knit brown and beige scarf, dark brown woolen overcoat, deep brown woolen stockings set into laced up brown leather walking shoes with a low heel, all of this topped by her brown umbrella as she went to mass and to do the grocery shopping. Seeing her no one would have thought that she was a happy woman. But Maria Assunta was.

Maria Assunta was married when she was seventeen soon to be eighteen. Marriage, she had known from her earliest childhood, was to be her destiny and so it came as no surprise to her when she stood at the altar in a white bridal dress, its hem a little longer and its train a lot longer than those on her communion dress when she became a maiden of the bride of Christ. Maria Assunta's parents had ordained that she should marry Angelo Belfiore, a distant cousin. Angelo's parents had agreed the two were a good match. Being the kind of boy who never saw reason to quibble with his parent's choices, Angelo joined his bride at the altar.

The two were married at the Holy Family Church, a monument like no other in the Rocky Mountains, built to the glory of God and the Holy Father in St. Peters. To receive the blessed sacrament of marriage in such a place assured the sacrament was sealed with a power so strong that Angelo and Maria Assunta did not question that sacrament.

It would not, in any case, have been in their nature to ask such questions. Maria Assunta had been a docile child. She was not cantankerous. She did not kick her parents in the shin when they made her eat salami. She did not bite her cousin Seppe when he pulled her hair. She dutifully prayed next to her bed on her knees each night, helped her mother in the kitchen and held her father's hand on the way to mass.

Maria Assunta attended school each day and was never late, nor was she early. She sat quietly in class and when asked a question would give a response which sometimes was correct and other times incorrect. She did not mind either way, since she did not see how the questions being asked were important to her. Had the teacher asked how to make tomato sauce or pizzele she would have been unhappy to have given the wrong ingredients, but since she was never asked, she never had to worry about it.

Angelo was a slightly plump, black haired and brown eyed boy who didn't like to talk much but who did like his mother's spaghetti sauce. More than anything else he liked to pray. He prayed when he awoke, he prayed before each meal and he prayed before he went to sleep. Sometimes he would pray, "Dear God, don't let the teacher ask me that question," and sometimes he would pray, "Dear God my father in heaven please let there be a Monopoly game under the Christmas tree." But mostly Angelo prayed to God, Mary the blessed Virgin and Jesus to look after his Mama and Papa and to make him a good boy. Being a good boy was very important to Angelo for he thought he might become a priest. He would talk to Father Barnes after Mass and ask him, "*Reverendo*, if I became a priest. Would I have to go to Africa?"

While his mother might have liked Angelo to become a priest she agreed with her husband when he said, "The boy will not become *un ecclesiastico!*" Though Angelo's father did not revere priests, this fact alone would not have led him to keep his boy from becoming one; rather he was dedicated to ensuring his lineage should be preserved and Angelo was an only child. For as much as his parents had excelled at the practice of trying to expand their family, their exertions did not provide Angelo with a brother or a sister. Thus the parents determined that their son and heir, Angelo, should be a bridegroom of a woman rather than a bridegroom of the Church.

When Angelo first heard that he would be married to Maria Assunta rather than to St. Peter he added an extra line to each prayer he made. "Please deliver me from this marriage." But as he never discovered that the power of prayer often requires a mortal push, and as he was an obedient son whose naturally meek soul did not have the power to stop his determined parents, his prayer went unanswered.

During the year before her wedding Maria Assunta liked to ride her bike. This was something she had liked to do since she was a little girl when her Mamma and Papa had bought her a little red bike with a gold crest and a Chief with a crown of feathers and the name Hiawatha on it. Sometimes when she was riding her bike she would repeat the name Hiawatha, Hiawatha, Hiawatha on each down stroke of the pedal. Riding her bike felt like flying. She rode her bike everywhere, to school, to mass, to communion class, to her Nonna's.

But it had not been easy to learn how to ride the bike. Her Papa had practiced with her, pushing her down the street while her Mamma watched. Papa would push yelling, "Pedal! Maria, Pedal!" And her Mamma would shriek, her hands in front of her face, "Careful! Maria!! Careful!" And Maria would peddle and wobble, wobble and wobble and fall. Her knees were scraped, her hands were cut but she would not stop trying until one day when her father let go she pedaled and pedaled and pedaled and did not fall. She pedaled all the way down the block. Then, not knowing how to stop, she kept on pedaling into the next block and her Papa ran all the way behind her shouting, "Stop! Maria, Stop!!"

"I don't know how," she shouted back, not daring to turn her head.

"Pedal backwards!" her father ordered. She did. She fell. Her father came to her grinning; he picked her up and gave her a big wet kiss on the cheek. "You did it, you can ride!" They picked the bike up and Maria Assunta got back on the bike and she rode it down the block to where her mother was standing. As she approached her mother clapped and laughed and cheered, though tears streamed down her cheeks.

When Maria Assunta grew taller she was given a new bike. There was no Hiawatha on it, which made her a little bit sad, but the fresh glitter of the pink and blue of the new bike made her forget her faithful chief. Though more festively coloured, her new bike was still a sensible bike, not a banana bike like the bad boys in her class mounted. She rode a sturdy CCM with a basket so that she could carry her books to school and deliver groceries to her Nonna and her Mamma.

It was easier for Maria Assunta to do the shopping than it was for her Mamma because Mamma's English was so bad while her Nonna had no English at all. Mamma and Nonna would give her a list in Italian and she would translate it and buy everything each needed. Her Nonna would say, "Maria is my *fattorina*." And they would laugh and her Nonna would give her a candy.

Maria Assunta would pedal through the streets of Fernie, the wind blowing in her hair, her fingers gripping the handle bars as the heavily laden basket tilted from side to side. She dreaded the pot holes which seemed magnetic and which sent her tumbling. She dreaded dogs even more when they gave chase, expecting cheerful play, but getting only shrieks of distress as she pedaled away from them as fast as she could.

Maria Assunta loved to cycle. She disliked the onset of winter because she could no longer fly on her bike and had to plant her feet on earth again and plod along like other mortals. In the winter she was still the delivery girl for the family but the bags were heavy and her boots were heavy. Though she loved to watch the snow fall and whip about in the wind, she felt she was bound to the ground. She looked out the window each day hoping to see the streets free of snow so she could get back on her bike.

As Maria Assunta's childhood began to tickle and then tear at the rough edge of puberty her blood began to warm. Her mother showed her what to do when her blood boiled over, which to Maria Assunta's annoyance happened as regularly as her mother needed her help to beat the carpets. It was when Maria Assunta was a pubescent girl her mother began to enlist her aid in rolling up the carpets, taking them outside, hanging them over the back fence and beating them. This ritual of cleaning occurred on the last Saturday morning of each month so that the carpets were clean for Sunday. These two happenings were inextricably linked for Maria because each in its own way was inconvenient and because each caused her to sneeze — deep spine twiddling sneezes. However, Maria did not associate the sneezing with her breasts which began to develop in a way that was pretty and pleased her. Mamma would say to Papa when they were alone at night, lying in bed, "Maria Assunta is becoming a woman." And Papa would nod quietly in the dark.

Maria began to enjoy her bike for the singular reason that depending upon where she mounted the seat a tingling sensation arose from time to time down there. She did not have a better name for down there, since nobody had ever told her what it was called; she just described it as down there.

The odd tingling feeling she found irritating yet at the same time pleasant, more in the recollection than in the event itself. Gravel roads were best for inducing the mysterious sensation and she would ride from time to time, on a Saturday if her housework and the weather allowed, out into the countryside around the town. Often she rode from the town out to Cokato and then on towards Morrissey. She would ride over the logging road to the Morrissey Bridge and cross the Elk River and then return home on the highway. When the flowers were in bloom she would stop in the meadows and fill her basket with daisies, buttercups, fireweed and Indian paint brush. Later she picked saskatoons and huckleberries or, if it were Autumn, she would gather boughs with colourful leaves and dried ferns and festoon the house with decorations. Her Mamma would complain, "I have to clean up all the petals that drop." But her Papa would say, "Let her Mamma, look how beautiful they are," and he would smile and stroke his daughter's hair.

It was the last sunny Saturday of August. Maria Assunta lay in bed as long as she could, hearing her mother's calls, "Maria Assunta get up, get up, get up. Let us do the carpets before the sun is too hot."

"Why don't we just buy a vacuum cleaner like everyone else!" she shouted back. But she knew that no matter how much she might chaff, the carpets would be beaten with the carpet beater and she would swing the intricately woven willow switches.

One by one they rolled up the carpets and carried them outside and hung them on the railing. One by one Maria beat the carpets while her mother washed the wooden floors underneath. The dust billowed and percolated and rose around her and she sneezed and sneezed. Her eyes watered and her nose ran and her skin itched, the sweat running down her chest and stomach and back. When each of the carpets was restored to the place they had come from and the furniture set back into the right place she shouted to her mother, "I'm going for a bike ride. See you later." Then, hopping on her bike, she sped off before she could hear her mother's reply.

She decided to ride her favourite route, out over Morrissey. The midday sun was high and the road was not shaded. She rode onward and wished she had remembered to bring a thermos of water. She stopped at the Coal Creek Bridge and walked down to the little stream so small that it, too, looked thirsty. She set her face close to the water and cupped her hands and drank a little. Then she continued, keeping watch for any brooks along the way. The late summer heat had dried them out. She rode stopping here and there to catch her breath. By mid afternoon she arrived at the banks of the Elk River at Morrissey. There she dismounted. Laying her bike in the tall grass, she walked out onto the big round rocks of the dry river bottom until she reached the ripples at the edge of the flow. She splashed her face, arms and legs with water and she drank placing her lips right to the water's surge; the water kissing her lips, her tongue caressing the wet.

The water was cold and good. With her clothes soaked and, her limbs, face and hair wet, she lay on the rocks and let the sun slowly warm and dry her and she fell into a reverie or even, for moments, a slumber. Then she heard laughing and shouting over the splashing of the Elk River. She looked up to where the sound came from. Afterwards she would never recall whether the figure had come from the sky or from the forest, although she clearly recalled the woman. A beautiful woman who wore a long white skirt that went almost to her bare feet and a pale blue wrap of cloth around her torso that started at her bosom and was knotted at the skirt. The face of the woman was serene even when it smiled and laughed as she stood on the edge of the water. Or did she stand on the water? Maria Assunta couldn't quite see. The woman unwrapped the blue cloth from around her bosom and belly revealing her breasts and flat white stomach. Maria, though surprised, was even more astonished when she realized she had seen that blue before. In fact she thought she knew the blue well. The woman continued undressing. She untied her skirt and gracefully let it slide along her legs. Stepping out from it she stood naked by the edge of the water, her toes wet. The woman stood for a moment, her eyes closed, then she opened them and her face radiated joy.

Maria Assunta watched as the woman levitated from stone to stone so that the river licked at her ankles. The woman bent over and splashed water onto her breasts, torso, pubis, thighs, knees, shins and then over her back. She laughed. Maria heard her speak, but did not understand her words. Maria Assunta was sure the woman was speaking in tongues unknown to her. The ecstatic utterances were punctuated with joyous exclamations. She heard but did not recognize words — "*Schön!*" "*Frisch!*" "*Herrlich!*" "*Toll!*" She had never heard such joy before. The woman's wet body glittered in the sun as droplets of water ran down her breasts and fell from the tips of her nipples, onto the curve of her frame. Then Maria noticed a crown of light. The woman had a distinctive golden halo that encircled her head as the sun caught and magnified the blonde hair that curled around her face and cascaded to her shoulders. In that instant Maria recognized her face. She had seen the face on the statue of the Altar to the Virgin Mary at the Holy Family Catholic church during every mass she had ever attended.

Maria Assunta shook her head and knew she must be

dreaming, but she could not look away from the beautiful vision. The woman walked towards her. Maria Assunta looked at her, paralyzed. She dared not even blink. She shook. The woman smiled at her, kneeled, bent over her and taking a handful of water slowly poured it onto her forehead. The halo was now so close to Maria's head that she could see the gossamer rays of light it emitted. The woman leaned into Maria's face and placed her lips onto Maria Assunta's. The woman kissed Maria Assunta. Their lips merely brushed, hardly a touch, and Maria Assunta looked into the deep blue eyes of the woman. Maria Assunta felt as she had never felt before: the rocks were no longer beneath her and her heart, stomach, womb, guts and blood longed to burst out, but, trapped by her skin, created a friction that blazed into heat that prickled her flesh so that it felt like butterfly wings were brushing her with dust that exploded. Then solace.

The woman lifted her head away from Maria and a few water droplets fell from the woman's face onto Maria's. The woman stroked Maria Assunta's hair once and with a flutter of her eyelids said, "*Wie schön Du bist.*" Maria Assunta felt blessed and her body relaxed into the stones on which she had been lying. She closed her eyes, pressing them shut. When she opened them again, the woman was gone. Maria Assunta lifted her head, looking about for the woman, but she was not there. The clothes, the halo, the lips, they were gone and Maria Assunta was alone on the banks of the Elk River. She began to cry and with each tear Maria Assunta said "goodbye" and the Elk River swallowed her words.

On the next day, Sunday, Maria went to early morning mass. She sat in the very front pew directly before the sculpture of Mary. She mechanically went through the recitations of the mass, all the while not taking her eyes away from the sculpture. She stayed seated after all the worshipers left. She rose. Slowly she walked up the steps to the base of the statue and lighted a candle, then she kneeled on the stair and looked up at the stone Virgin. She stayed on her knees and looked. She did not pray. Father Barnes, preparing for the next mass, thought she must be in prayer. He wondered if Maria was troubled, if he should speak to her. But her face looked happy so he did not disturb her. When her knees grew sore she sat on the edge of the steps. She did not stir until she heard the arrival of the sleepy pious for the late morning mass. Again she took her seat in the first pew. Her mother and father, as was their custom, came to this mass and they sat down next to her. Her father on her left and her mother on her right.

Her mother whispered, "Maria?"

Maria looked at her with the same quiet contented smile she had had all the previous evening at dinner and after. Her father just patted her arm.

Throughout the second service she remained transfixed by the Virgin. But the stone did not stir, and she walked out of the church holding on to her father's arm. In the days after, Maria Assunta stoically helped her mother in the house. She went to school, she went to mass, she went to visit her grandmother. She said little and mostly replied with her enigmatic smile. Her mother spoke of it to the priest, and at the next mass he asked, "Maria, it's been a while since you've been to confession?"

She entered the confessional determined to tell the father what had passed on the banks of the Elk River. She kneeled and began the incantation, "Bless me, father, for I have sinned." As he blessed her, she began to tremble and wanted to run out of the confessional. But she pinched herself and told herself she must go on. So after making the sign of the cross she said, "I confess to Almighty God, to Blessed Mary," and here she stumbled for a moment and stuttered the words, "ever Virgin, to all the Saints, and to you my spiritual father." In that moment she realized that she could not share the bliss she had found on the banks of the Elk River with a mortal; with a man such as the priest. She continued, "that I have sinned." She followed with the words, "I was at confession two weeks ago; by the grace of God I received absolution, performed my penance, and went to Holy Communion," and as she said those words she had said so often she remembered something she had done that she could tell the priest.

"I told my cousin Pina a lie. I told her all good Catholics have to sleep facing Rome so that if they die in the night the Holy Father in Rome will see them and bless them on their journey toward heaven."

The priest chuckled to himself since this explained why little Giuseppina had asked him (when he had visited her ailing great-grandmother) what would happen if her Bisnonna turned over in bed in her sleep and didn't face Rome.

He heard Maria Assunta finish, "for all these sins and for those I do not remember." She hesitated and the priest tilted his head, for he knew that at this moment some of his congregation would tell him the real reason they had come to confession. But Maria, in that pause, was suddenly sure that what had happened to her was not a sin but a blessing. She smiled, the big toothy broad smile of those whose heart is suddenly light and said loudly and with gusto, "I ask pardon of God with my whole heart, and penance and absolution of you, my spiritual Father."

Maria Assunta did not hear what the priest said after that. When he had finished talking she rose from the confessional, walked up the aisle and standing before the statue of the Virgin said, "Thank you."

2

On her wedding night Maria Assunta put on her new white cotton night gown. Her mother had sewn it with ruffles around the bodice and the hem was trimmed in pink stitches. It fit loosely but not uncomfortably and it gave Maria more of a feeling that she was married than had her wedding dress. She combed her long dark hair and lay down in the bed and waited. "Mrs. Belfiore, I am Mrs. Belfiore. I was Miss Belfiore and now I am Mrs. Belfiore." She laughed nervously as she thought about Angelo who was gargling in the bathroom. "Mr. Belfiore. Mr. and Mrs. Belfiore."

Her new husband came into the bedroom. He sat on the edge of the bed and placed his watch on the little night table, before he turned the bedside lamp off. Maria heard the bed sheets rustle and the springs uncoil as he arose from the bed. She heard a creak of the floor and she realized that Angelo was on his knees beside the bed. She heard him whisper as though he were a child telling his mother a secret. When she heard what she knew was "Amen," she realized he had prayed. Then he stood up, pushed aside the sheets and comforter and he lay down in the bed beside her. In the dark she heard him say, "Good Night." The room was still and in a few exhalations she knew from his regular breathing that he had fallen asleep. Maria's eyes widened as she looked up at the black above the bed that stretched to the ceiling.

She imagined the stars that watched over the house and she sighed.

Every morning Maria Assunta would awake alone in the bed. The house would be silent. She would hug herself. Then she would arise, pat her face with water and vigourously brush her hair, put on a day dress and go into the kitchen, where she would pull the espresso pot from its shelf and make a coffee. If it was Saturday or Sunday she would not stop in her kitchen. She would continue into the back yard past the vegetable garden, out the gate, across the alley and into the house where she knew that her mother-in-law and Angelo would be waiting for her at the breakfast table. But for the stillness of the bedroom each night, her days were like the days of her mother, her mother-in-law and their mothers before them. She easily accustomed herself to the cadence. In the first days of marriage their family and friends would gently tease them about making babies. Angelo and Maria Assunta would blush, but as time passed and there was no evidence that a child was likely, the jokes faded and finally disappeared. There were whispers that Maria Assunta might be barren.

The snowflakes had at first drifted down in a desultory meandering fashion as though the clouds were undecided about whether or not to share their burden with the pines, spruces, browned ferns, grasses. The trees were mostly naked but for a few leaves that mimicked prudery. Maria Assunta looked out her kitchen window at the house of her mother-in-law across the alley. The paint was peeling. Where the wood siding was bared it was black from the days of autumn rain and sleet that seemed unending. The snowflakes were a relief. Maria Assunta leaned on her kitchen sink and prayed for it to snow and white wash the drab. By midmorning, when she was walking over to her Nonna's from the post office, it was as though the clouds had heard her prayer and the snow began to fall more heavily. The flakes became corpulent. By noon her foot prints embossed the walkway up to her house door. Inside she made a tuna salad sandwich and a cup of tea and sat on the arm chair watching the snow fall. Curled up in her arm chair she fell asleep.

She was startled by a knocking noise. It was forceful. The knocking seemed intent on being heard. The knock came again. Her front door. She raised herself from the chair. Her legs stiff. She stumbled. Patting her hair she looked out the little window of the door. There she saw a man who looked at her with expectant eyes and a warm smile. She opened the door enough so that she could see him properly. His head was uncovered and snowflakes were melting into his tawny hair so that they flattened the long loose curls into cords of gold that framed his face and joined the light beard at his ears. He grinned broadly. His full lips pulled back as he smiled to reveal a very straight line of white teeth.

"Can I shovel the snow off your walk, miss?"

She squinted at him.

"Only five dollars." He grinned again.

Her head began to turn, to signal no, but her eyes caught his. She thought how warm and brown they were, like pistachios, molasses and honey.

She smiled at him and tilted her head, to inspect him more closely. She liked how he looked and she felt herself wanting to have him shovel the walk. But five dollars was a lot of money and she knew she couldn't really afford it. Besides it would cost her nothing if she shoveled the walk herself.

"I don't have five dollars," she said. This statement was true. Maria and Angelo kept all their money in the bank and only took out what they needed.

He looked at her, his grin relaxing into a smile.

"I have two dollars, I think." She thought about the coins.

"I'll be glad to shovel your walk for two dollars, miss."

He turned and started by pushing the snow off the steps. Maria watched him for a moment, then went into the house to her little coin jar and poured the coins onto the kitchen table. There were six quarters, three dimes, four nickels and seven pennies. She was relieved. Taking her coat and hat from the hook by the kitchen door and putting on her boots she went out to the front porch and leaned against the pillar that held the hand rail up the steps. She watched the man shovel the snow.

His movements were quick and efficient, his arms moving like the rods of pistons revolving on their bearings. Each stroke, lithe and graceful, bespoke strength. He pushed the snow to the edge of the walk and then lifted it and threw it high to scatter it onto the snow that covered the lawn. It was a movement he repeated over and over making his way down the walkway from the steps of the house to the boulevard where the walkway joined the sidewalk. At that crux he stopped and looked up. He rested his arm on the top of the shovel handle in a way that reminded Maria Assunta of a Greek statue the art teacher in the school had shown the students. "It is by Praxiteles, the greatest ancient Greek sculptor," the teacher had said, and she did not forget this fact because the beauty had made her feel shame.

He turned to the house where she stood on the porch. He grinned, it was the same grin that had encouraged her to part with the two dollars she had saved from her kitchen money. She wondered if he was telling her he was done, that he would not do the sidewalk for the two dollars.

As though reading her thoughts he grasped the shovel

and began on the sidewalk. He worked his way to the right border of her garden. Reaching it he stopped, looked back and saw that she was still watching him. He saluted. It was a slight movement, his black mitten tilting towards his head as though to remove a cap. The gesture made her smile.

He walked back towards the unfinished stretch of sidewalk. His gait had a slight amble and, if it were not for the feline grace of the movement, he would have appeared to be cocky. He stopped to wipe his brow with the sleeve of his coat, then, leaning the shovel into the heavy snow, he began scooping it aside. Maria Assunta's eyes followed the rhythm of his hips cantilevering back, his arms pushing, lifting, tossing, propelling the snow from the end of the shovel. She saw, for the first time, that a man at work was beautiful.

The idea that a man was beautiful puzzled Maria Assunta and caused her to feel uncertainty, an uncertainty that started in her stomach, like a nausea caused by too much tiramisu. It spread down from her belly and wound its way through her intestines past her hips and into her legs. Suddenly she felt that her legs would give out. She turned, took a stride, gripped the door handle and pulled herself around the door as she opened it. She sank to the floor just inside the door. From there she peered out at the shoveling man.

"What are you doing? Why are you being so silly?" she whispered. She breathed heavily and deeply, her nerves tingling. Then she shouted, "Get up! Get up!"

She saw that the man was finished shoveling snow and was walking back towards the house. She saw his eyes were searching for her behind the slightly ajar door.

Maria Assunta pulled herself up by the door handle. She felt a little dizzy. The man was standing on the porch looking in at her. She pulled the door more open so that half her body was visible to him. She knew he saw fear in her eyes.

He said, "Are you all right, miss?" For the first time she noticed his voice. It was a rich baritone and had a kind timbre.

She nodded. "Won't you come in while I get your money?" She wondered if her neighbours would notice the stranger going in her house door.

"Sure."

She opened the door and stepped back.

He kicked off his boots and then came through the door and stood in the sitting room. She noticed how he looked around slowly, politely, with his eyes, not his head. She saw that he wore heavy grey woolen socks with a red toe cap on each foot.

"Why don't you sit down?" she said.

Silent, he took off his jacket and laid it on the floor next to the door.

"You're not from Fernie, are you?"

"No, I'm just here for the winter. You know, to ski." He laughed, "and shovel snow, I guess."

She had heard of these young men who came to Fernie to ski, but she had never met one. She had never even been to the ski slopes. She thought it must be exciting to be such a man.

Perhaps because of this and because she only had two dollars she asked, "Would you like a cup of tea?" Then she told herself, I should just give him his money and send him away.

"That would be great. I'd love a cup of tea."

I can't send him away now, she thought, and then said, "I'll just put the kettle on."

Maria Assunta sidled into the kitchen trying to keep an eye on him. He sat looking up at the mantle on which was hung a picture of the praying hands of Dürer and a small statue of the Virgin Mary. She put the kettle on the stove, her fingers clumsy, as though it were she who had shoveled the snow. She rubbed her hands to still them and took out her best teapot. She had two: a brown betty and one of white porcelain with pretty pink wild roses. She pulled out the matching cups and saucers. She laid them on a tray and placed a matching plate next to them on which she placed some pizelle.

She felt his presence and turned toward the sitting room. He had moved into the doorway behind her. This startled her and she leaned back against the kitchen counter.

"Sorry," he said.

She blushed. He walked over to her and stood beside her looking out the kitchen window. The snow was still falling. "I'll have to shovel it again before I go."

She could smell the lightest scent of him. She sniffed. She recognized the smell of musk in the air on a hot summer day in the big cottonwoods down by the Elk River. She leaned in. She sought him.

The kettle whistle screamed and she pushed away. He smiled at her and she blushed. He took the kettle from the stove and brought it to the tea pot. She pulled a box of Red Rose from the cupboard next to the sink. As she handed him two bags their fingers touched; she was surprised by the heat. She wanted to rest her hand on his but willed herself to let go of the teabags.

He pursed his lips as though a cherub, "Only in Canada, You say? Pity...." She laughed, her nerves still singing from the feel of his fingers.

Later, much later that afternoon, as the sky darkened, she wrapped her housecoat tightly about her breasts and again watched him shovel the walk. He did it with the same easy economy of movement as the first time. He finished at the far end of the garden, then, turning for a brief moment to look at the house, he walked down the street.

Maria Assunta felt a peace and vibrancy she had last known in her childhood. It stirred a memory of sitting on a pew in cool shade under the spans of arches in church looking at the stained glass windows and for the first time seeing how the tinted glass beamed as the sun carried the colours to her eyes. Dazzled, her head dizzy, she sat down on the sofa.

His passion had been ardent but tuned to her own melody as though he had known her for a long time and was pleased to carry her along on his own bass notes. He expressed no surprise that she was a virgin and with patience and forbearance he helped her to avoid distress. She was surprised that she felt no modesty, no embarrassment and no discomfort as this man, this stranger, touched her in places she never touched, kissed her where no lips had been. Though at first she shivered, she opened to the heat of his body. For the first time she felt a yearning to fold herself around a man — this man. She tangled her fingers through his long gold hair, she bit his lips and pulled on his beard with her lips. He laughed and kneaded the muscles on her back so that she shuddered and arched into him. Their animation became more urgent. His gentle manipulation became assertive and she thought she was beginning to lift from the bed. She felt as if she was on her bike — no hands, no feet, coasting down a mountain slope, brushing past daisies. She remembered a sunny afternoon on the Elk River. Then she felt an exhilaration and a crest of joy so alarming that she began to cry even as she bubbled and gurgled with laughter at her release.

He was quiet, stroking her hair, her breasts, her belly with round gentle motions. His fingers trailed her tears and he put them to his lips. She smiled. He kissed her on the cheek. He rose from the bed. She watched as he pulled his underwear up, put on his trousers, his shirt, and then sat on the bed, crossed one leg over the other and tugged his socks on. He turned to her, smiled and kissed her stomach. "Gotta go." He walked out of the room and she heard his feet on the stairs, light, not like the thud of her husband. The house door closed and in a moment after he had gone down the stairs, she heard the scraping of a shovel against pavement.

She pulled her arms through the sleeves of her house coat and wrapped it tightly about her body. The flannel reminded her of his touch. She went down the stairs and stood beside the sitting room window. She looked out at the white street and saw that he had finished clearing the walkway and was working on the last stretch of sidewalk. She looked at his muscular movements and she began to think he was an abstraction. As though he had never really been with her at all, as though it had all been a dream. Yet in her lap she felt the secret and knew it was real. She marveled that beyond a warmth and relaxed sleepiness and a deep contentment she felt no sin, no shame.

He pushed the last of the snow from the sidewalk. Looking back at the house for a brief moment he tilted his head as though saluting, then turned and walked down the street. Her eyes followed him until he disappeared in the falling snow. She sighed and thought she should bathe but she did not. She dressed and began preparing for dinner.

That night, after Angelo and Maria Assunta had sat silently throughout dinner, she went out and shoveled the snow from the sidewalk. Angelo watched television. She came back into the house and as she took off her coat she said, "I'm going to bed." Angelo did not turn to look at her as she placed her boots on the mat by the door.

She did not put on her nightgown. She lay down in the bed; her naked torso shivering against the cold of the sheets. She could smell him, his musk. She gently stroked her breasts, belly, thighs, her pelvis, and she felt warm.

As though called, Angelo came up to bed earlier that night but beyond that he did not vary his ritual. She listened as he brushed his teeth, gargled, spat. She heard the stream of his urine, the flush of the toilet, the sound of water running, the clang of the pipes as the tap shut off. He came to the side of the bed, took off his watch, placed it on the night table and turned off the light. Then she heard his whispered litany. Finally he lay in the bed and said, "Good Night."

She sat up. She turned to Angelo and in one swift motion she straddled his groin. She hissed, "Angelo, make love to me." Angelo's body became stiff and she heard him splutter. She undid the buttons of his pyjama shirt, she ground her pelvis into his groin. She felt him responding. She rocked more gently and gave him space. Then gripping him she replayed what had happened in the bed only hours before. Angelo did not move, his body taut as though in the grip of a seizure, but she did not notice. She relived what she had lived in the other man's arms and it did not matter that Angelo's body was an unwilling tool. It did not matter that Angelo repeated the mantra over and over, "God our Father in heaven forgive us our sins, Mary Mother of God forgive us our sins, Jesus forgive us our sins." Maria Assunta was in that moment for herself and when Angelo ejaculated she kept on until she felt release. Then she lay back on the bed and immediately fell to sleep.

3

Maria Assunta sat in front of the statue of Jesus that stood under the arch to the right of the Altar and looked up at his face. She did not often think of the stranger who had shoveled her walkway, but at unexpected moments she would remember him. She couldn't really recall what his face looked like. Time had blurred it so that she sometimes thought she recognized him as a television actor in one of her soaps, or as one of the skiers walking past as she worked in her garden. At the end of a ski season they were muscled from a winter on the mountain. In quiet moments in church she thought he might be like the statue of Jesus, though his hair had been much shorter and she still thought of the Greek sculpture, though she could no longer remember the name of the sculptor.

Maria Assunta did not often think of her visitations because she no longer often thought of herself. All her thoughts were for her son. This change had begun when she felt the first movement of his body inside hers. She had been surprised by the first stirrings in her womb, but once she became accustomed to them she began to speak to the child. She would hum or sing and tell him all the things she was doing. She would tell him about her Mamma and Papa and Nonna and sometimes she would even mention Angelo. When she walked down the street she would say to her growing belly, "The people, they are all looking at you, especially that nosy Angelina. How she used to laugh at me that I didn't have a baby."

Maria Assunta remembered feeling proud as she walked down the street and people looked at her belly. It was big.

People pointed and smiled. Some of the women who were even more audacious touched her.

Her Nonna was more circumspect and would not rub her belly, so Maria Assunta held her Nonna's gnarled hands in her own and placed them on the womb. Her Nonna said, "It will be a boy."

"I don't care whether it's a boy or girl."

Angelo said, "I hope he's a boy."

Her father and mother said, "So long as the child is healthy, nothing else matters." And she knew they meant it.

Her Nonna was right — the baby was a boy.

When the nurses took her son away to be wiped clean and weighed, Maria Assunta felt a new kind of fear, the fear of a mother. She wanted to yell, "Don't take him." But fatigue and embarrassment prevented her and minutes later when the nurse brought him to her she was glad she had remained quiet.

She held him. She looked at him again and again. He was not as pretty as she thought a baby should be, but then she had never seen a newborn before. It was not until she began to nurse him that she saw his profound beauty and from that moment on she never saw a child who could compare to the beauty of her son.

Now she felt proud that the boy was in his first year of university. Both she and Angelo had been devoted to their son. Everything she cooked had been made with extra care because her son would eat it. She ironed his clothes with precision so that even the underwear had sharp creases. She saved money from her shopping allowance to buy him special things. Angelo, too, was untiring in his desire to show his love for the boy. Though Angelo himself had never worn skates he bought his son a pair and took him to the arena so that he could skate with the other boys. He showed him how plants grew in the garden, though he never asked the boy to dirty his fingers. Every day he said, "Son, one day you will go to the university. You won't have to work with your hands like I do." Maria and Angelo tried not to spoil the boy, though the grandparents and Maria Assunta's Nonna valiantly defended their right to pamper him.

The boy blossomed and grew despite being fed too many bowls of gelato, receiving too many toys at Christmas, and despite being hugged and kissed too much. He loved his mother, his father, his grandparents and his Nonna and tried to be good. When he became a teenager, the girls in school began to notice him. Though he was somewhat placid in nature like his parents, he did take advantage of his black hair, his careless grin, and his sparkling eyes. Maria Assunta and Angelo worried that the boy would have girl trouble so they took him to a doctor. Maria Assunta sat waiting with her son while Angelo went in to speak to the doctor.

"Why are we here, Mom? Is something wrong?"

Maria Assunta blushed, "You wait, nothing is wrong, the doctor, he's going to talk to you."

Angelo came out, smiled sheepishly, and rubbed his hands. "Son, you go in and see the doctor, he wants to have a talk with you."

The boy went into the doctor's office while Maria Assunta and Angelo sat side by side not saying anything. When the boy came out, he grinned and looked at his parents with a mixture of amusement and adoration but he didn't say a word. As they walked towards the North End where they lived he took them each by the arm and they all knew that he was a man.

In the first days after her son left for University, Maria Assunta thought she was losing her mind. She had never been separated from her son for even a night from the morning of his birth until the day he had disappeared in the car that was to drive him to Calgary to the University. She felt his absence continually. Had she looked into Angelo's empty lusterless eyes they would have told her that her husband felt a similar pain.

The two sat in the house in silence and waited for Angelo to come home for weekends. Then there was such joy in the house that they both could not stop talking and laughing and asking their son questions about the university and the city. They would go for walks around the neighbourhood and Angelo would say, "Hi, Mrs. Saccomani, you remember my son, he is at the university!" They would walk on proudly till they met another neighbor and Angelo would say, "Salve Signor Triossi, here is my boy back from the University." And thus he would repeat the phrase adjusting the name to the recipient of the news. Those were the happiest days of the year for Maria Assunta and on those days she would remember the feeling she had on the day he was born when she lay in the hospital and nursed him.

She would remember how he had suckled the first time as she gazed at him and said to her husband, "Angelo, his name is Donatello, our gift from God." And Angelo, thinking of the moment of conception, agreed.

A LITTLE TEA AND SOME JUSTICE

Mrs. Arthur Young had the custom of shopping three times a week. Mondays, Wednesdays and Fridays she would make her rounds as early in the morning as the shops would open. Putting on her sensible shoes, or if the weather were cold her fur lined boots, fur lined coat, and gloves as required. She would place her little folding umbrella into her wicker basket and she would walk from her house in the Park down Victoria Avenue. She walked the Avenue in summer noting the state of each garden and remarking whether or not the lawns had been recently mowed. In winter she noted whether the snow was properly shoveled from the walkways. If it was not before December 13th she was happy to see the Christmas tree all ready, but if it was after January 6th she would cluck her tongue if a tree were still in the living room window. She did not remark upon the state of the mountains that encircle the town because she felt that God looked after those and to comment upon His gardening skills was presumptuous.

If she met anyone along the way she would greet them with a resonant, "Good Morning!", and like her attire, she would vary the remainder of her salutation to suit the weather so that the hearer might know, "Fine day we're having" or "Foul day we're in for". If she did not care for the person the "Good" was dropped and the recipient of her regards knew that at least it was "Morning." They were left to their own consideration of the state of the weather. In this fashion she walked to that part of Victoria Avenue where the shops line the street.

Over the years all her purveyors and close acquaintances came to know that she would visit the baker first, then the butcher, after that came the department and general stores, where she bought her hardware, pharmaceutical, dry, canned and green goods followed by any number of the little shops — the shoe maker, the haberdasher, the dressmaker — which lined Fernie's main street. Mrs. Young was known to examine a product at the Trites Wood Co. Store and compare it with the same product at the J. D. Quail Hardware or the Crowsnest Trading Company. For groceries she would visit the MC Cash and then see if Metro had it and if she found them wanting in price or quality she was known to make a purchase "at the competition" as she called it.

Such fickle allegiance was not the case with the baker and the butcher. There was, to her mind, no competition when it came to the baker. Regarding the butcher — though there was the Bairns Meat Co., or, as it was more commonly known, Martinelli's, where shrewd old Louie and his men stood behind a long gleaming counter in long white aprons brandishing long knives — she preferred to patronize Fernie Quality Meats. There she relied upon brothers Eddie and Bobbie Brown who stood behind the short counter and were proud to say all their beef was "tender as a mother's heart." The veracity of this statement of course had never been tested. It was up to the patron to determine how much poetic license (or tenderizer) might have been applied to the steaks, briskets, roasts and chops in the establishment.

Mrs. Arthur Young refused to purchase at Martinelli's because the wife of that good butcher had once made a snide remark about a hat that Mrs. Young wore to church. Some of her friends caught wind of this and the remark reached Mrs. Young's ear, who remembering her Christian duty, forgave the butcher's wife but did not forget the unkindness and thereafter never patronized Martinelli's again. It was her view that if the wife of the man selling the beef was unkind so, too, would be the cut of the steaks.

There was another reason Mrs. Arthur Young patronized Fernie Quality Meats — she knew this is where she would meet her friend, Ivy Greenleaf. It was the custom of Ivy Greenleaf to shop on Mondays, Wednesdays and every second Friday. The other Friday morning Mrs. Greenleaf stayed at home with a mop and bucket because that was the day Greta came "to do the cleaning". Mrs. Greenleaf spent the morning before the arrival of her cleaner ensuring the house was spotless so that no account would circulate in the town of any untoward (ungodly) untidiness in the "manse" as she liked to call her little house next to the church where her husband preached.

Mrs. Greenleaf was not as particular about her beef as was Mrs. Young, but she liked to patronize the Brothers Brown because the first thing they asked after greeting her when she walked into the butcher shop was, "What's new?" Whether or not either Eddie or Bobbie expected an answer was not known, but it was certain that Mrs. Greenleaf viewed this as an invitation to lean against the meat counter and begin a discourse on the news of the day as reported by her friends, parishioners and Greta.

Thus it came that early one frosty sunny Monday morning, just before the last potatoes had to be dug out, Mrs. Ivy Greenleaf propped her ample bosom against the counter of the Fernie Quality Meat Market inspecting, with more care and attention than usual, the cut of the pork chops. She listened to Bobbie take the telephone order from the Trites Wood mansion. It was not without interest that she noted each item, and thought, there must be visitors at that tony residence. She had heard that the eldest daughter might be in town with her new husband. She also listened as Mrs. Campbell, wife of the school teacher, told Eddie to slice the meat more thinly, no doubt to economize. Engaged as she was with the task of inspecting meat and the meat of others, Mrs. Greenleaf was startled when the little bell above the door tinkled as the door opened and her dear friend Mrs. Arthur Young walked in, her silver gray hair marceled and peeking out from an elegantly knotted scarf, her prominently boned cheeks glowing red from the cold morning air.

Mrs. Greenleaf looked up and greeted her friend casually, "Why hello Violet." Mrs. Greenleaf betrayed a slight frisson of electricity in her tremolo which she tried to disguise as interest in Mrs. Young's scarf, "What a darling scarf you have!" She moved towards Mrs. Young and her fingers reached for the silk swirl of autumn leaves in brown, red and gold that framed her friend's face. "Is it new?" she exclaimed. She pushed up her own home dyed and permed brown hair with the hope that it was not too frizzy from the damp morning air.

"No, don't be silly Ivy," smiled a pleased Mrs. Young, "I've had this old thing for years."

"It so becomes you my dear," said Mrs. Greenleaf, her voice softly quavering. The tone alerted Mrs. Young and whether it was the inflection of the "it" or the "dear" Mrs. Young knew that Mrs. Greenleaf was going to tell her something. News Mrs. Greenleaf hoped that Mrs. Young did not yet know. News the Brothers Brown also did not know. News Mrs. Young expected Mrs. Greenleaf would only part with after a little dance ensued between them.

By this time the Messrs. Brown were no longer engaged with either the teacher's wife or the telephone and they turned their attention to the Mesdames Young and Greenleaf.

"Good Morning Ladies," boomed the big voice of Eddie. Bobbie merely nodded, and said, "Ladies," believing his brother had greeted the two heartily enough.

"Good Morning, Bobbie, Ed," responded the duo in dulcet tones of menopausal femininity. Both sang in the church choir — Mrs. Young soprano, Mrs. Greenleaf mezzo.

"What can we do for you?" asked Eddie.

Mrs. Arthur Young, as she always did, began to place her order with Bobbie. Mrs. Greenleaf likewise placed her order with Eddie. Mrs. Greenleaf bought her usual two pork chops, one five pound pork roast and ten slices of salami. Mrs. Young ordered an eight pound rib roast and a piece of tongue as she was going to make an aspic. This was not her usual order and Mrs. Greenleaf made a mental note to ensure that she ascertained why the order had varied. She wondered if the Youngs might be entertaining. And as she had not received an invitation, puzzled over who the guests would be.

She might have pursued this topic almost immediately but for the certain rule that news untold becomes a burden to the teller. Mrs. Greenleaf was not one of those rare exceptions to this rule and this morning she had news to tell. She had entered the shop with the expectation that she might have an opportunity to share some of her news with Mrs. Young in the presence of the brothers Brown. She had counted on letting out a little clue when one of the Browns asked "What's new", but this they had not done. She was further agitated because Mrs. Young did not ask her how the weekend had been. Consequently it was becoming more difficult for Mrs. Greenleaf not to blurt out her piece of news.

The foursome chatted about the weather. It had been a long Indian summer and each ventured to guess when it might break. Mrs. Young stated, "The boys haven't got all the storm windows up yet, and one of them is broken, so it might as well stay nice till that's done."

"Quite right, Violet. I could stand a little more time to get all the carrots out of the ground. But no doubt the weather'll change in the Lord's own good time." Mrs. Greenleaf liked to lean on the Lord when she needed to push for weather reprieve.

Eddie, a fatalistic friend of the weather as it appeared out the shop window, rather than how it might turn out, nodded grimly. But Bobbie being an eternal optimist opined, "It's like the fall when the Buck boys drove off the road and into the Bull River. T'was sunny right until the week before Christmas."

The brother's tabulated each order, placed the amount on the ledger of each of the ladies' accounts, and then wrapped the meat. It was then that Bobbie, noting that no new customer had joined them asked, "What's new?"

Remembering the intonation of the "it" and the "dear" and noting the excited look in Mrs. Greenleaf's eyes, Mrs. Young lunged into voice, not giving her friend a chance to speak. "Oh nothing much new really, Ethel Preston was telling me the Rylands have had another little one, a boy this time. I don't know how many that makes, but one wonders how Edna Ryland can do it?" She did not say at her age, but she did add, "and how they feed all those mouths really worries one." Mrs. Young smiled thinking how her old classmate, once one of the beauties of Fernie Secondary, looked surrounded by her brood. Eddie's and Bobbie's eyes drooped with boredom. This was not news; they had already heard that the Rylands were up to nine children from patrons all day Saturday, the birth having been Friday afternoon.

Mrs. Greenleaf who normally had much to say about the Rylands and their propensity for children remained silent. She rocked ever so slightly from foot to foot, not so much that one could see it, but so that her skirt and overcoat swayed. She looked expectantly at the party but Bobbie and Eddie sensing and Mrs. Young recognizing Mrs. Greenleaf's desire to share something remained silent. It was a part of the Fernie manner not to appear to indulge gossip gratuitously. The shop was still for a moment too long. Mrs. Young inclined her head knowing that her friend could not hold out for long.

She was right. Mrs. Greenleaf finally, as calmly as she could, expelled, in the fashion of air being let from a tire, the words, "I have news." Then she paused. Her desire not to betray relish and to remain ladylike before her three listeners forced her to concentrate on evoking a reserved tone that almost caused her to choke and made her words lugubrious. "There was a fight down by the river last night."

She looked at her listeners with ill-concealed delight. Her audience, no matter how interested, should have appeared impassive or possibly disdainful of someone who directly declared they had news. Here was news they had not yet heard combined with violence. Mrs. Young inclined her head, the nostrils of her fine but long nose sniffed and her angled eyebrows arched ever so slightly but the glint in her eyes betrayed her interest. The Messrs Brown clucked at each other and finally Bobbie said, "That'll be why the police siren woke me up." His house was just up the hill from the Elk River.

Mrs. Greenleaf, determined not to be interrupted, picked up the thread. "Yes, the police were there, it must have been bad. The Reverend got the call to come to the hospital."

Mrs. Young arched her right eyebrow even more as her left resumed resting in the wrinkles around her eye. She asked, "Why the Reverend?"

"Well," Mrs. Greenleaf paused. "You know the Reverend never talks about our parishioners and so I don't know for sure, but you may guess that there was only one reason they would have called him at 11:30 at night when we were already lying fast asleep in our beds. It nearly gave me a heart attack when the phone rang." She paused for breath.

Her listeners, if asked, would have questioned the confidentiality of the Reverend, though he was more careful than many, because Mrs. Greenleaf was sometimes careless and in subtle ways let confidences slip without knowing she had done so. It was the case that Mrs. Greenleaf was intuitive — she built her talk about others by putting together the chatter of the town with her knowledge of the whereabouts of the Reverend. Her deductions made her right more often than wrong when it came to happenings in Fernie.

Eddie and Bobbie knew it was better for business if they let their customers draw conclusions and pronounce them, so Eddie wiped the counter of the meat display and Bobbie leaned on the broom with which he intended to sweep the floor. Neither opened their lips. Mrs. Young stood still wondering if Mrs. Greenleaf would state the obvious and in this she was not disappointed.

"You know they only call a man of the cloth to the bed of someone at 11:30 at night if that someone is about to die."

Mrs. Arthur Young realized that, as much as she might like to, it would be crass to ask who it was that the Reverend had attended to. And this thought, prompted a further thought. Mrs. Young had heard enough to realize that her friend was about to embarrass herself and the Reverend in front of the butchers. So with a smile that hinted at the *schadenfreude* she felt at denying the Brown brothers any more of the news, she brusquely said, "Dear me, look at the time, I really must be off. So much to do today. Ivy, dear, won't you walk with me. I've got to stop in at the Trites Wood store." She picked up the packed meat and placed it in her basket.

Mrs. Greenleaf puzzled and somewhat perturbed, knew that she had been given a cue by her friend. She also knew that if she did not follow Mrs. Young she would be left standing alone in the butcher shop when she had more news for Mrs. Young. Prompted by her friend she picked up her package and turning to the door, which Mrs. Young held open for her, the two women bid the meat purveyors, "Good Day."

They walked side by side. Mrs. Young, tall and thin, strode with a brisk dignity beneath her tailored autumn overcoat that flared from her svelte waist. Being more squat and round, Mrs. Greenleaf had to walk quickly to keep up. They moved up the street past the ornate Bank of Commerce. Mrs. Greenleaf said, "Isn't the sale at Trites's already over?" She tended to economize by shopping when things were on sale.

"Why, of course, dear, but I need some silver polish. Little Nettie's got to do the silver today and we're almost out." They walked past the even more ornate Roman revival Hydro building. Mrs. Greenleaf was in a consternation. She was certain that Mrs. Young was going to have visitors, but she also had to finish telling her news. Mrs. Young was about to turn into the entry that led to the big double doors of the Trites Wood department store when Mrs. Greenleaf stopped, touched her friend's arm and said, "Little Nettie probably won't be in to work today."

"What?" asked Mrs. Young, "Why won't Nettie come to work?"

Mrs. Greenleaf leaned into Mrs. Young and whispered, though the street was empty, "It was Tommie Jackson that they called the Reverend to see."

Mrs. Young breathed more excitedly, her eyes taking on a glint of alarm. Mrs. Greenleaf congratulated herself at being able to astonish her friend, twice in one morning.

"Are you sure?"

Mrs. Greenleaf nodded, her face grave.

"Oh dear," sighed Mrs. Young, "Poor Nettie" and she made a face, sad though with a flicker of irritation, because if Nettie didn't come to work that day she would have to polish the silver herself.

Nettie Jackson was christened Annette Marie Fletcher. She was the youngest of the brood that Beryl and Fred Fletcher had raised. Nettie was the baby of the family and the darling of her parents and all her five brothers and three sisters who had indulged her as much as is possible when a large family lives in a two bedroom cottage.

The Fletcher family lived in a cottage because they were miners. The boys all followed their father Fred Jr. into the mine. Fred Jr. had followed his father Fred Sr. into the mine and it was likely the grandfather before that had come from the coal pits of England, though no one could remember for sure. Beryl had come from a mine family, too, and the girls all but for Nettie, like their mother, married miners.

Nettie had married as she liked to say somewhat rebelliously, "A man who works in the timber industry." Her mother referred to her youngest daughter's husband as, "That no good for nothing lumberjack." Her father had an even more colourful name for her husband, which he muttered under his breath each time he saw his son-in-law.

Conversations between Nettie's father and mother about their daughter, when it came to the subject of the suitability of the son-in-law, would always end with Beryl saying, "See that's what comes of you spoiling the child," though she had been as guilty as the rest of the family of giving in to Nettie's wishes when it cost no cash.

Fred's aversion to his son-in-law had been immediate upon hearing the boy's last name. Fred did not approve of Jacksons; if asked he would not have reflected why. It was just so. "Fletchers never like Jacksons let alone marry them," he had railed, when his daughter told him she was going to be marrying Tommie. His antipathy, nay loathing, became firmly fixed in his heart and mind at the wedding banquet on the day when his daughter took Tommie Jackson to be her lawfully wedded husband before the Reverend Greenleaf.

Mrs. Greenleaf attended the ceremony and provided some of the flowers and, as was the custom, she and the Reverend were invited to the wedding supper. The Fletchers being of the parish and Beryl Fletcher attending church dutifully each Sunday, the Greenleafs had felt it their Christian and professional duty to attend the dinner to celebrate the wedding. As Mrs. Greenleaf told the Reverend, "We'll save the chops for Monday." And the Reverend being aware that no other invitation to dine had come their way, and like his wife, being mindful of economies, agreed.

Thus it was that Mrs. Greenleaf was able to report as much as she knew to Mrs. Young about the wedding. Mrs. Young had listened, out of general interest in the town doings, while she did her needlepoint. It was, if she investigated her own motives, why she had invited Mrs. Greenleaf to tea when she had seen her at the butchers the Monday morning after the wedding.

"My dear," began Mrs. Greenleaf sipping Earl Grey tea

from Mrs. Young's second best china as they sat in Mrs. Young's everyday sitting room, "you know I was at the most extraordinary wedding on Saturday."

"Oh," said Mrs. Young. Mrs. Greenleaf wondered if she detected boredom but ignored the tone and continued.

"That Little Nettie Fletcher was married to Tommie Jackson. And can you imagine, the bride was six months pregnant if she was a day. I mean she looked becoming in her gown, as best she could, but it was there plain as day. I felt so sorry for Beryl."

"Who is Beryl?" Mrs. Arthur Young could forget the names of people not of her own circle.

"Why dear, Beryl is Nettie's mother. You know, Beryl Fletcher. She is such a sweet woman, so patient, though a little lacking in energy. You may be sure she is worn out from bearing and bringing up all those children. And that husband of hers, though they say he is a hard worker, is very slack at attending services." Mrs. Greenleaf's idea of magnanimity being to judge the lesser parishioners on their attendance at church more than by their general contributions to society.

"I think Beryl, though she put on a brave face, was mortified that her youngest should march up to the altar looking like a brood mare. Her father made no pretence, he frowned throughout the whole ceremony. Tommie's parents looked pleased as punch, and rightly, if I may say so; maybe Nettie'll be able to settle that boy down."

"Perhaps," said Mrs. Young, her tone dubious. "Those Jacksons are a wild bunch. I don't' think the father Jackson is any better than the son."

"Mmmm." Mrs. Greenleaf hoped she sounded contemplative, but Mrs. Young heard affirmation.

"Do go on." Mrs. Young hoped to hear something more interesting than this tidbit.

"The ceremony was lovely. The Reverend gave a beautiful sermon about how love affirmed in matrimony was a union that led to a strong foundation for children. I really think it helped Beryl feel more comfortable with Nettie conceiving out of wedlock. The Reverend is so forgiving about these things, a real man of God you know. As long as there's a wedding, he says, the first child can come at any time, all the others take nine months."

Mrs. Young was not prone to splitting theological hairs. As she liked the Reverend, she was not inclined to argue the niceties of whether or not a conception in or out of the state of wedlock was to be viewed as being something needing forgiveness. She was, however, pleased that the circumstances of the wedding confirmed her own view that the working man, be he miner or lumberman, could not be counted to attain the moral rectitude that was expected in her own circle. But then, as she did not claim to know any miners or lumbermen, this was a prejudice that she formed from such tidings as were chatted about in the houses of her acquaintanceship or could be gleaned from the pages of the *Fernie Free Press*.

Taking a sip of her tea, Ivy Greenleaf continued. "After the ceremony we all went downstairs into the church hall where the supper was laid out. They decorated it very prettily too: pink and white flowers made of tissue and streamers in pink and white and white paper table cloths. The ladies catered it and the Fletchers made a very nice contribution to the collection for new hymnals. There was turkey and ham and roast beef. Potatoes and peas and carrots, and thank goodness, Libby East made her Jello Fruit Salad. It's the only one I can abide, and there was Ambrosia. Beryl baked the wedding cake and decorated it very nicely, too."

Mrs. Young noticed that the word "ladies" and not

"ladies guild" had been used to refer to the catering. Mrs. Young had been asked by Mrs. Greenleaf, many times, if she wouldn't consider leading the "ladies guild". Mrs. Young was, however, not inclined to be placed in a position that she might be in charge of catering weddings such as that hosted by the Fletchers. It was not that she felt that all charity must arise from the cheque book, but she did feel there was a limit that could be asked of someone such as herself. As it was she preferred to sew little handiworks which the guild could sell at their annual tea and craft fair. Besides, Mr. Young liked his wife to host dinners for select citizens of the town and this she felt was enough effort on her part when it came to catering.

"I thought," continued Mrs. Greenleaf, "the toasts went rather well. At least there was no mention of the bride's state. After that the bride and groom had a little dance to music played by Vinnie and Guido Costanzo. Beryl told me her husband wouldn't stand for music by the Wops but she said in the end they had to have the Costanzos because they weren't able to find anyone else. I am sure she meant they couldn't afford anyone else, so the Wops it was, but perhaps I am being uncharitable." The Costanzo brothers played the piano, accordion and violin creditably and could, when asked, play more than the tunes which they had brought with them from Italy.

Mrs. Young, to soothe her friend's quibbles about charity, smiled, and said, "I am sure you are quite right my dear."

"Well, when the dancing commenced it really was high time for the Reverend and me to leave, but you can't imagine what happened next. We had just been saying our good-byes and I had told Beryl what a lovely wedding it was and she thanked me so very sweetly. But we hadn't yet said goodbye to the bride and groom or the father of the bride. Beryl told me they had all gone out for a breath of fresh air. So we thought it a good way to leave. We were coming up the stairs from the hall when we heard a real hullaballoo outside the church doors. The Reverend rushed forward, telling me to stay inside, but I had to go out and see that the Reverend was alright. You won't believe me when I tell you I was in such a state. "

Mrs. Young smiled to herself. She could well believe that Ivy Greenleaf had been in a state, for it was known to all of their acquaintanceship that Mrs. Greenleaf was prone to excitation.

"There on the ground before us were the father of the bride and the groom wrestling and punching and yelling. Fred Fletcher was on top and was hitting the groom about the face and shouting, that Tommie was a no good for nothing lout. Though he used a stronger word. And that he had gotten his Nettie pregnant and that he was a disgrace. And Nettie, well she was pulling on her father to try to get him off Tommie and she was screeching like a banshee, that he should "get the hell off". It was most unladylike and not only that, it looked like the bodice of her dress was torn and I thought I saw blood on the skirt, but then Tommie was bleeding from his nose. It really was dreadful." She paused for breath, her eyes fiery, and Mrs. Young could see that her friend was still shaken by what she had witnessed.

To comfort her friend she said, "My dear it really does sound quite dreadful."

"Oh, but that isn't the worst of it." Mrs. Greenleaf inhaled loudly before continuing. "The Reverend tried to intervene! He kept saying, 'Come now Gentleman, Come now, surely we can settle this amiably, 'tis a wedding.' And Fred Fletcher said, 'Give over Reverend, I'm going to teach this vermin a lesson he doesn't soon forget; knocking up my daughter and then making a joke of it.' The Reverend then said to him, 'Come on Fred, we can't have this ruckus at your daughter's wedding. Look at her. Gentlemen, you're spoiling her day!' And just as he leaned over to try to disengage the men he was struck by the back of Fred Fletcher's hand. Not that he meant to hit the Reverend. He was raising it to strike Tommie again. The Reverend tumbled, I must have screamed, for the two of them stopped wrestling, and Fred Fletcher got up and went over to the Reverend, who was stretched out on the grass. I ran over to my dear husband and Fred Fletcher began to apologize profusely, though I thought I heard a snicker at first."

Here she gathered breath and added, "The Reverend must have been knocked cold because, as he came to himself, he looked at me and said, 'Good Morning Ivy.'"

Mrs. Young couldn't help smiling as she imagined her friend's pompous husband laid out on the church lawn but she merely nodded and said, "My goodness."

"Fred Sr. helped me get him up and we sat him on the stairs. Poor, poor Beryl, came out of the church hall. She had tears in her eyes and she just kept saying over and over, 'Are you alright Reverend, are you alright.' And Fred said, 'Oh come on Mom, of course he's alright, he's a man, and a man like the Reverend, he can take a little tumble.' Which whipped me into a fury so that I yelled, 'Fred Fletcher, you are a brute. And at your age to be wrestling with your son-in-law. No better than savages.' I thought for a moment that he laughed, so I gave him a look such as he'll not soon forget and he shrugged his shoulders and slunk off, though I swear he was laughing. Beryl just kept apologizing over and over and some of the people came up from the hall and there was quite a crowd and it was horribly humiliating for Beryl so that finally I said, 'Beryl just calm yourself. The Reverend's okay. Aren't you dear? Let's be off; I'll get him home.' And so with the Reverend leaning on my arm we walked back to the manse and I put the Reverend to bed. I could hear Beryl scolding Fred and her daughter and Tommie, though I think he drove off in the honeymoon car."

Mrs. Greenleaf paused. "This morning I was talking to Willa."

Mrs. Young frowned slightly at the reference to the ladies guild president. "What did that busybody have to say about it?"

Mrs. Greenleaf, clucked under her breath at either Mrs. Young's disapproval of Willa Caruthers, who though perhaps a busybody did not, like Mrs. Young, think herself too grand to be ladies guild president. Or too grand to hear what she was about to say next. She smiled and almost chuckled, "Well Willa said, that Beryl went back downstairs into the hall. Apparently she stood in the middle of the assembled guests and said that they were all to go home. It would seem everyone did, and then Beryl, to her credit, thanked Willa and the ladies of the guild for having done such a wonderful job of the food and asked if they would mind if she did not stay to help with the clean up. Of course Willa told her it was okay and she walked Beryl to the door of the hall and told her to go home and have a cup of tea and not to worry about anything. The ladies of the guild would clean up the hall. I feel so sorry for Beryl I thought I'd visit her tomorrow after she's had a bit of time. I mean imagine that, to have such a fracas at the wedding when the bride is already in disgrace."

Mrs. Young looked over her reading glasses, she could no longer see where the needle went without them, and gave her friend a penetrating glance. Then with a tone of finality she said, "Why should they make such a fuss, isn't that how half those girls end up getting married?"

Mrs. Greenleaf nodded almost imperceptibly and then sighed. If asked she would have had to deny the sentiment as being unchristian, but in her heart she agreed with Mrs. Young who was of the view that in certain neighbourhoods of the town, and especially where the miners lived, propagation was a more certain route to matrimony than was love. Mrs. Young would, if pressed, have gone on to argue that the multiplication of children in those rougher parts of Fernie, whether by accident or love, was also a certain route to destitution. In either belief it would have been hard to challenge her since she would point to the logical evidence that in the households in West Fernie, the Annex, Little Italy or the North end, where there were many children, there also seemed to be want. Whisperings of shot gun weddings were common.

"Shotgun wedding," those were the words that all the town applied to the nuptials of Little Nettie. Some of the townsfolk, particularly those who had attended the wedding, had laughingly said that it was lucky that Fred Fletcher didn't have a gun that night or it might have been a post-wedding shotgun affair and Tommie might not have lived to see his first child born. Others said Fred had managed to mete out an adequate lesson on Tommie with his fists.

The two ladies did not further develop the subject of Little Nettie's wedding that afternoon, nor did they chat about Little Nettie or her wedding again, until Mrs. Greenleaf would mention that another child had been borne to Little Nettie. She did this by telling her friend that the Reverend would be welcoming a newcomer into the congregation with a christening and that the newcomer was a child of Little Nettie. Then the two friends would smile and exchange a quiet look and Mrs. Young would say, "How many does that make now?" And Mrs. Greenleaf would know with precision because it was her view that her husband's success in the eyes of God was linked directly to the number of parishioners he had in his flock — a death being a loss of an asset and a birth being an accretion. Thus she could provide the number of children in each family in the parish.

It was on a drive back from the Crowsnest Pass where the two ladies had undertaken to do some tax free shopping, in Blairmore, on one of the clear snow free days shortly before Christmas that Mrs. Greenleaf announced, "The Reverend will soon be christening number four for Little Nettie and Tommie Jackson."

Mrs. Young was driving with careful attention in the big black Oldsmobile that her husband had recently purchased and would have preferred she not drive at all. She did not speak until she was round a tight curve on the road. "Well it looks like their rocky start doesn't seem to have affected them in the baby making department. Don't tell me they're going to breed as many as the old man did. How many did what's his name have?"

Mrs. Greenleaf viewed her friend's failure to remember names to be uncharitable and therefore she harrumphed and added just to be difficult. "Violet do you mean Fred Sr. or Fred Jr.?"

Unmoved by the annoyance in Mrs. Greenleaf's voice, and wondering if there would be ice on the road by Crowsnest Lake, Mrs. Young answered, "What, there's two of them?"

"Come now Violet, you know Fred Sr. is Nettie's grandpa, and Fred Jr. is her pa."

"Well, whichever one of the two has the more children is the one I mean."

"That's Fred Sr. for sure, he had twelve but Fred Jr. and Beryl have nine."

Mrs. Young smiled in a way that someone less familiar with her face than Mrs. Greenleaf might have considered malicious, "So Fred Jr. not only inherited his father's name but also his propensity to sire children. Though I suppose he'll have to spawn another three if he's to rival his father's fruitfulness." She paused worried by the semi truck and trailer that was approaching down the pass behind her car. She did not care to share the road with other motorists especially not these large "road hogs" as she called them. She slowed the car and pulled towards the shoulder as much as she could until the truck had passed, gravel hitting her car, so that she inwardly groaned, wondering if there would be any marks on the finish for Mr. Young to complain about. The truck safely ahead of them she returned her attention to the conversation and added, "I suppose at Beryl's age that's unlikely though." And the two women chuckled, the laugh kind, for they were relieved that the truck had moved away and pleased that they too were past bearing years.

It was not long after that Christmas that an unsettling event occurred in the life of Mrs. Young. The carefully constructed calm of the Young household was disturbed by the news that Mrs. Christine Cornfield, the housekeeper of many years, was leaving to retire to the home of her son in Saskatoon.

Years back, a newlywed Mrs. Young had hired Mrs. Cornfield to help her in the house and the two had tolerated one another ever since. Mrs. Cornfield liked to be called Chris, and when there were no others present referred to Mrs. Young as Violet. Mrs. Young frowned on this liberty but never felt she could complain since she had been a very young bride when Mr. Young had brought her to their house in the Park. Chris Cornfield was as jolly as she was robust and, beyond telling people she had lost her husband in a mine explosion, she never referred to herself as a widow. Mrs. Young never praised the work that Chris did, though as a housekeeper she settled into a rhythm of domestic cleanliness that was reliable and this reliability was extended to the care that Mrs. Young allowed Chris to give the two Young children until they left Fernie for university.

The news of Mrs. Cornfield's departure shocked Mrs. Young, but not so much that she couldn't think to herself, "Now I can hire someone who can really clean the way I want." Though what she meant was that she would ensure that the new housekeeper would call her "Mrs. Young" all the time. Chris Cornfield had offered to have her neighbour come to work for Mrs. Young. However, Mrs. Young determined that she would find her own replacement. So within the day of the unsettling news there appeared in the help wanted columns of the *Fernie Free Press* the following frugally priced announcement: Housekeeper wanted, part-time, live out. Call 6008.

Each of the first few days after the advertisement was posted Mrs. Young would wait for the telephone to ring with the hope that it was a candidate for the position. She became troubled that the phone should be even more quiet than usual. By the third day after posting the advertisement she decided she would talk to her friend Mrs. Greenleaf about the matter. She and Mr. Young were dining at the home of Mr. and Mrs. Trites Wood, and when the ladies were leaving the dining room to men and port, she casually mentioned to Mrs. Greenleaf, though she thought it might be bad form, "My housekeeper is leaving me and I can't seem to find another one."

Mrs. Greenleaf grimaced, she didn't like it when Mrs. Young referred to her cleaning lady as a "housekeeper" but she knew that her friend's reliance on Chris was more pronounced than her own on Greta so she merely said, "My dear, that is bad news. Whatever will you do? I'd suggest my housekeeper but she's already too busy."

Mrs. Greenleaf felt she had her revenge, though she would have been enraged had she known what her friend thought of her use of the appellation "housekeeper" for Greta who was a mere cleaner.

Mrs. Greenleaf proceeded to drink her coffee and think about how she could help her friend and Mrs. Young sat and feigned rapt attention as Mrs. Trites Wood, the doyenne of Fernie, told of her recent visit to friends in Calgary. When Mrs. Trites Wood was done, and after the gentlemen had joined the ladies and the coffee was finished, Mrs. Young and Mrs. Greenleaf determined that it was time to go home. Coats were gotten and goodbyes exchanged with vigourous shaking of hands and kisses of cheeks. Mr. Young and Mr. Greenleaf, followed by their wives, walked down the drive of the grand house where Mrs. Trites Wood reigned. This gave the two friends a moment to exchange words.

"I think I know someone who can help you," whispered Mrs. Greenleaf, as though afraid that Mrs. Trites Wood might hear her speak of domestic issues.

"Oh?" returned Mrs. Young softly.

"Yes, I think that Little Nettie would be perfect."

"Who?"

"You know, Little Nettie, the Fletcher girl."

"The one with the wedding ruckus?"

"Yes, that one," said Mrs. Greenleaf with a snicker. Wine often helped her to forget she was a Reverend's wife.

Mrs. Young ignored the vulgar sound and asked with a serious tone, "But doesn't her husband drink?"

"I don't think more than most loggers. And they need

the money, the logging is so unsteady and they have so many mouths to feed."

"Do you think she can clean?" Mrs. Young had not ever been inside any of the smaller houses in town but she felt with certainty that they were generally not cleaned adequately. If pressed she would have admitted she made that judgment based upon the attire of the children who played in front of those houses.

Mrs. Greenleaf pulled on her friend's arm so that they stopped as they passed through the gates of the drive and said, "If she can't clean then teach her, it's the only charitable thing to do, they really need the money. The children haven't enough to eat. Let me send her to you tomorrow." She did not add that Little Nettie had appealed to the Reverend for a loan to help make ends meet.

And thus Little Nettie started as a part-time live-out housekeeper in Mrs. Young's employ. Mrs. Young had Chris Cornfield show Little Nettie how to make the beds, scrub the floors, clean the toilets, arrange the table linens, and all that miscellany of cleaning and caring for a residence that is required of a housekeeper. On Chris Cornfield's last day Mrs. Young hosted a goodbye lunch in the kitchen for her departing housekeeper, which also worked nicely, she thought, as a welcome lunch for Little Nettie. Mrs. Young even made the egg salad and ham and cheese sandwiches herself and bought fresh baking from the bakery. She gave Chris Cornfield a nice Timex watch as a memento of their time together and the two women parted company with tears in their eyes. Mrs. Young and Little Nettie returned to the kitchen and the hostess accepted with a gracious and pleased smile when Little Nettie said, "I can do the washing up Mrs. Young."

Mrs. Young was so pleased with Little Nettie, that on

her next visit to Mrs. Greenleaf, she said, "My dear Ivy, what a treasure you have sent me in Little Nettie. She is simply wonderful. I showed her how I wanted things done and she has been doing the job better than that Chris Cornfield ever did. It has made my life so much easier."

"And you were worried that she wouldn't measure up," said a relieved Mrs. Greenleaf, for she had feared that a failure on the part of Little Nettie would be viewed by Mrs. Young to be a failure on her own part. She was also pleased because she hoped that her ability to bring house and housekeeper together would help the struggling Nettie without costing her anything.

Mrs. Young remained pleased with Little Nettie's work, and so after a time they settled into the harmony of mistress and servant. Mrs. Young always felt that Little Nettie's work was especially good on those days she called her "Ma'am".

Within a few months Mrs. Young began to pay no more attention to Little Nettie than she had to Chris Cornfield, which is to say that she noticed that Little Nettie didn't always set the toilet paper the right way round on the paper roller, the way Mr. Young liked it, or that the corners were not dusted right into the corner, or the sheets not ironed so that when unfolded there were box like creases. She would say to Little Nettie, "Now Nettie I don't like to complain, but …." and then the omissions would be pointed out. She would finish with the words, "And I know you can do better."

Little Nettie would respond, "Yes Ma'am" and for a few days there would be no complaint from Mrs. Young and Little Nettie would sigh with relief when each work day was over.

Then there came a day when Mrs. Young noticed that Little Nettie was quieter than usual, and that her eyes were red and that her hand trembled as she brought Mrs. Young a cup of tea. They were sitting at the kitchen table so that they could go over the list of chores for the day. Mrs. Young, her eyes squinting slightly, looked at Little Nettie and asked, "Is everything alright Nettie?" To which the younger woman replied, "Oh fine Mrs. Young, just fine." And Mrs. Young, though not convinced, was relieved as she feared that Little Nettie might be hung-over.

Mrs. Young did not approve of drinking beyond the sociable glass of wine or sherry and though Mr. Young might sometimes indulge in a tumbler of scotch, the Young household, while not temperate, was moderate in the consumption of alcohol. She had heard that there were women in the town who were alcoholics and turned a blind eye to some in her own circle. However, she was not prepared to abide a housekeeper who took to drink, and she made a point of checking the bottles in the liquor cabinet for a few days each time after Little Nettie left the house.

It was less than a week later that Mrs. Young again noticed that Little Nettie's hand was trembling, and her eyes were red. This annoyed Mrs. Young and she determined to examine her housekeeper more carefully. She was just about to say, "Nettie you don't seem to be yourself today, is there something wrong?" when she noticed that over the whole of Little Nettie's face was applied a heavy layer of what looked like powder finer than flour but with a tone that mimicked flesh. This powder coating, had it been white, might have given Little Nettie the appearance of a geisha, but being more pink, it left her face with a hue so flat that all dimensions disappeared. Mrs. Young was very puzzled by this and she contrived to look at Little Nettie's face more closely.

Little Nettie usually started by washing the breakfast dishes and any dishes that were left from the night before. It was Mrs. Young's habit, if she and her husband dined alone, to place the dinner dishes in water to soak overnight; this she reasoned lightened the housekeeper's load in the morning. The very odd time, when Chris Cornfield had worked for her, she had helped to dry the dishes as a way to speed the work up if there were much to do, but beyond that she usually left the kitchen after speaking of the day's requirements. She determined that she would help with the dishes that morning. To Little Nettie's surprise, she said, "Nettie I'll dry. We have a lot to do today."

She placed herself next to Little Nettie at the sink so that the light from the window over the kitchen washstand would shine onto the young woman's face. Then she said, "So how are your children?" Mrs. Young felt it was safe to speak to most women about their children and she thought Little Nettie would be no different. In this she was correct; Little Nettie seemed pleased and relieved and said, "Oh they're so good. My Tommie Jr. is just starting school and he seems to really like it. He does such a fine job looking after the littl'uns when Sally Markam can't. She's my neighbor in the apartments. Sometimes my Mom helps out, but Tommie, that's their daddy, doesn't like it so much when I take the kids round there."

Little Nettie turned, her eyes glowing with the natural love a mother has for her children, the red surrounding the blue iris highlighting the joy her children brought her. She smiled as she said, "My Evie she's as pretty as a lady bug. She's starting to walk. Toby, he's my other little boy, he's into everything, but he's a good boy. The baby, she's so sweet, hardly ever cries. My Mom says she looks just like me when I was a baby." Little Nettie laughed at the thought and as she did so she leaned towards the window.

In the grey March morning light Mrs. Young saw that

under the face powder there was a dark splotch next to Little Nettie's left eye. Though she had not often seen a black eye she knew there was the unmistakable bruise of an eye that had been hit. She looked more closely and thought — though her eyes were not the best — that she saw, in the moment before Little Nettie turned her head away, there was also a bruise where the cheek joined the jaw.

Mrs. Young continued drying the plate she held and then in as smooth and calm a voice as possible asked, "And how is your husband Tommie?"

Mrs. Young was sure she saw a slight flutter of Little Nettie's hand but Little Nettie replied, evenly, "Oh y' know, it's hard being a logger. Work's kinda uncertain."

Little Nettie, her face cast down to the dishwater as though she were looking for something in the water where her hands rested, said, "That's why I appreciate you taking me on Ma'am."

Mrs. Young smiled, and putting down the dishcloth she patted Little Nettie on the arm and said, "I'm glad dear, I'm glad." Then, realizing the affectionate nature of the gesture and feeling rather embarrassed that she had been too familiar with her helper, she said, "Dear me look at the time. We really have much to do today. I must be moving along." And she walked out of the kitchen leaving Little Nettie bowed over the sink.

Mrs. Young briskly went up the stairs to her bedroom and sat down at the little writing table she had in the bay window that looked out over the garden. There she stared out the window at the dreary sky where a little sleet was falling onto the snow that still lay heavily over the lawns and flower beds. She rubbed her hands as though there were too much night cream on them. She was sure Little Nettie carried the marks of a beating. She knew she dare not ask.

Somehow she felt that she would hear Little Nettie say, "Oh I hit my head on the cupboard" or something like that, so a question would be futile and would lead to further embarrassment for them both.

She was not sure what she should do about the image that she now conjured as the reason for Little Nettie's bruises. She knew that it ran contrary to every belief she had with regard to how a woman should be treated. Men might fight in Mrs. Young's world, but by that same code no man must ever strike a woman. Mrs. Young was offended for all womanhood by what she suspected had occurred to Little Nettie, but being offended and being able to do something about the matter were two different things. Mrs. Young also had a strong sense, learned from her mother, that a wise woman steers clear of the matrimonial disputes of others and thus she convinced herself that this matter might best be settled within Little Nettie's milieu.

Determining that the matter of Little Nettie's bruises was a subject to be resolved by her own kind was something that Mrs. Young felt would best be achieved by talking about the bruises to her friend Mrs. Greenleaf. On the next occasion when they met she raised the subject.

They were at a baby shower being held by Mrs. Trites Wood for Mrs. John Brookes. As was customary each of the women had given two dollars towards a big gift and then they all brought small tokens to the shower as well. The gifts were all arranged on a table in the centre of the grand sitting room. Little tables and chairs had been placed in the room so that the ladies could sit in fours at each or they might sit on one of the sofa's and use a coffee table to hold their cup, saucer and cake plate.

Mrs. Young firmly took her friend by the arm and said, "Ivy dear, why don't we sit together." To Mrs. Greenleaf's surprise Mrs. Young did not lead her to the table where Mrs. Trites Wood and the expectant mother were sitting and where she had wanted to sit. Rather Mrs. Young led her to the settee that was positioned in front of the fire place that could fit but two and was adequately remote from the other tables that their conversation would be private.

When they were seated, their backs to the room, Mrs. Young keeping her tone quiet though casual said, "Ivy the Reverend must occasionally encounter matrimonial frictions in his line of work?" Mrs. Greenleaf's eyes opened wide, she was not sure she understood Mrs. Young's query but she knew that their tea conversation was going to be more interesting than usual.

Mrs. Greenleaf looked at Mrs. Young with unconcealed wonder, "What do you mean matrimonial friction?"

"Well you know, dear, when a couple isn't getting along so well?"

Mrs. Greenleaf's eyes squinted; she whispered, her voice excited, "You and Arthur?"

Mrs. Young laughed, her cut-crystal chortle underlining the sparkle of her eyes. She was genuinely amused that her friend would think that she and Mr. Young would have matrimonial difficulties. They had been so long settled in their respective roles of husband and wife that there was nothing to be difficult about. However, had it been the case, and this she found the most absurd, the last person in Fernie she would have told would have been her friend and the Reverend.

"No, no dear," she smiled fondly, as though she were patting a favourite child on the head.

"But who then?" asked Mrs. Greenleaf just as titillated to know the identity of a third party as she was by the idea of Mr. and Mrs. Young.

"Little Nettie and her no good logger."

"Oh, why do you think that?" Mrs. Greenleaf did not disguise her interest.

"Well, the other day I noticed that she had coated her face in makeup, and when I looked closer I saw what looked like a mark."

"What do you mean a mark?"

"You know. A dark patch."

"How do you mean a dark patch?"

Mrs. Young felt frustrated, she did not like to use a word that was so blunt as to directly imply the violence that she was referring to, but her irritation at Mrs. Greenleaf's inability to grasp what she meant led her to blurt out, "I mean a shiner."

Mrs. Greenleaf was perhaps not as foolish as Mrs. Young might at times think, yet she said, "Violet dear you don't mean…"

"Yes, Ivy, I mean a black eye.

Mrs. Greenleaf smiled with self-satisfied interest. She had the view that most men were brutes to be tamed by the Church and by women. She often said, "I'm glad I have married a Lamb of God." Though in the early days of their marriage she might have preferred the Reverend to be a little more amorous. She felt that her marriage, but for this one deficiency, was exemplary. If the Reverend left her in large part alone in the bedroom, he was an unfailing gentleman everywhere else. He left her largely unhampered by demands other than that his dinner should be on the table punctually and that she should sit properly attired and listen to him reverentially both in church and out.

Mrs. Greenleaf looked at her friend and said, "I wouldn't be surprised." She shook her head and then nodded. "Did you ask her what happened?" Her curiosity exceeding the thought that it might be unladylike to enquire.

"Of course not Ivy. How does one ask something like that?"

"True, true. But if you didn't ask how do you know it was from her husband?"

Mrs. Young knew her friend to be naïve at times, but this, she thought, was too much and her voice though quiet became piercing, "Ivy what sensible woman covers her face with makeup to hide an honest bruise. No, she looked like a woman who was beaten."

The room hushed, the ladies had heard a sound amiss, but were not sure where it came from. Mrs. Trites Wood rose from her table and walked over to the sofa on which sat the Mesdames Greenleaf and Young. Standing with her back to the two friends she announced. "Ladies, ladies, it is time for the bingo. The special prize is a mixing bowl set donated by our store." Then turning to Mrs. Young and Mrs. Greenleaf, her tone sharp, she said, "Ladies, would you be so kind as to help me by giving out the bingo cards." The two friends not sure if they were censured smiled graciously at Mrs. Trites Wood and quickly stood up to take the bingo cards from her and pass them around to each table.

Mrs. Greenleaf and Mrs. Young were prevented from further conversation that afternoon. They telephoned later that evening and spoke of the matter once more before each retired to bed smug with the thought that their husbands wouldn't raise a hand to them. Mrs. Young had concluded the subject with the words, "And if he ever did, first I'd hit him back and second I'd leave him and that would be the end of that."

The next day was the second Friday of the month and thus Mrs. Greenleaf's cleaning day. The matron of the manse spent the morning tidying the cupboards in the kitchen because it was Greta's kitchen day.

It was also a cleaning day on which Mrs. Greenleaf was able to sit in with Greta for tea. After the work was done she told Greta to put on the kettle. While Greta filled the kettle with water she took down the Brown Betty tea pot and two Red Rose orange pekoe tea bags and handed them to Greta before going into the pantry. The pantry was a small room that was poorly lit because the Reverend had put in the lowest wattage of light bulb. He feared the waste which occurred when a light was left to burn in an unattended room. Mrs. Greenleaf had grown accustomed to finding things by feel and so she pulled out a pound cake that Willa Carruthers had given her earlier in the week. The pound cake and tea being placed on the table, and a mug and plate before the two women, Mrs. Greenleaf hardly waited for Greta to have her apron off before she said, "Greta, how is little Giesbert?"

"Ach the boy is so sweet, he has such a good heart, he tried to save a little robin that was hurt yesterday, but his Opa had to kill it and he cried all the afternoon. But what could we do. The little thing flew into the window and broke its wing."

Greta had come to Canada from Germany after the war. It had been her idea to come and she had convinced her husband, son and pregnant daughter-in-law that they would have more opportunity in the new world. Not long after their arrival in Fernie Greta's son was killed in a mine accident. The daughter-in-law soon gave birth to a boy who she left with Greta so that she could go to Calgary to find work. In Calgary she found a job and soon a new Canadian husband who was not interested in looking after the son of her first husband. Since that time Greta and her husband had been mother and father to little Giesbert. Greta was not unhappy about this though she often said, "Ach Mrs.

Greenleaf that woman was no good. What kind of mother leaves her child?"

Mrs. Greenleaf knew there was a danger in asking Greta about her grandson. Such a question could lead to story after story of how gifted the boy was though he seemed very ordinary to Mrs. Greenleaf. She cut Greta off with a question that would more quickly lead to the place she wanted the conversation to go.

"Does he still play with that little Tommie Jackson?"

"Ach," Greta shook her head, her face troubled, "I don't know what to do, the two boys they fight more then they play. That little Tommie he is turning bad like his father. I try to find nicer friends for Giesbert but it is hard." She did not add, for a German immigrant, but Mrs. Greenleaf knew that this was what she meant. Greta continued, "I don't push too hard though, because Beryl, his grandmother, is so kind to us when we come to Fernie and she is my friend. And it is a problem that we live in the same apartment house that they live in too. I think that no good for nothing papa of the boy puts him up to fighting with Giesbert."

"It could be, it could be," nodded Mrs. Greenleaf.

"Well you know we hear that papa he screams much it makes me want to cry."

"Do you think he, you know, does more than that?" Mrs. Greenleaf could not bring herself to say the word but raised her eyebrows willing Greta to understand.

Greta's head tilted in the way that made Mrs. Greenleaf think of her dog, Otis, catching a scent.

"What you mean?" Greta was one of those German's who prided themselves on being direct.

"Well," Mrs. Greenleaf stumbled, "I mean, oh you know." And she nervously made a light clap of her right hand over her left hand.

Greta's eyes opened a little wider.

"Ach, I don't think so, they scream much at each other, but I don't think he hits her."

"Well you know dear I heard she had make-up on and people are saying it was to cover bruises."

"What is a bruise?" Asked Greta puzzled.

"You know, a black mark from being hit." Mrs. Greenleaf rubbed her cheek as though she had been struck there.

"No, that would be terrible. Poor Little Nettie. It can't be."

"I agree dear, but you never know, do you."

Greta nodded her head. She knew from experience with her own father that beatings could be hidden well, and she sought to change the subject.

The two went on to discuss the church Strawberry Tea which took place every spring and for which all kinds of crafts needed to be made. Greta was a very handy woman and Mrs. Greenleaf enlisted her aid in ensuring the craft stall was well supplied with knit and crocheted things that Greta had made and little wooden sculptures that Greta's husband had whittled.

Mrs. Greenleaf was genuinely fond of Greta and enjoyed chatting with her so the afternoon passed quickly and soon it was time for the Reverend to take his tea, making it time for Greta to leave. The Reverend did not dislike Greta. Rather the Reverend struggled with his past when he saw Greta and this made him awkward in her presence. The Reverend had been borne a *Grünblatt* — a name associated with many tears and that had been changed to Greenleaf at the start of the Great War. The family had seen difficult days. The Reverend had watched his mother go off to clean the houses of others after the Great War. As a result he felt kindly towards German immigrants such as Greta, but his frugal nature prevented him from taking joy in paying for that kindness. Thus Mrs. Greenleaf and Greta, to avoid the odd behavior the Reverend exhibited whenever Greta was present, lessened those opportunities from arising. Greta always left as the Reverend arrived so that their relationship was largely one of "Hello" and "Good Bye".

Mrs. Young hosted a bridge evening once a month to which she invited her bridge ladies. These card-playing women (when not planning church teas for the guild) were known to hazard cutthroat rubber bridge at one another's houses once a week. It was natural that among the circle who were invited to play was Mrs. Greenleaf. The Reverend was not convinced that it was appropriate for his wife to play cards. However, as she slept with a copy of *The Bridge World* next to the Bible on her night stand and as the other ladies were of the guild he kept his concerns largely to himself. Of course he did not mind that it gave him a free evening as well.

On bridge days Mrs. Young and Mrs. Greenleaf arrived early to help one another prepare for the party. They would arrange a refreshment table with cookies and squares and coffee and tea and the two ladies took pleasure in assisting one another. Mrs. Young often thought there was more work to do at the manse than at her own home likely because she kept Little Nettie late in order to help set up the card tables. Before the other bridge ladies arrived Mrs. Young and Mrs. Greenleaf would sit down to a light supper. As was usual Mrs. Young found a way for Mr. Young to dine out on bridge nights. This was easier than might be presumed because the husbands of the other bridge players also sought amusement amongst themselves. Often Mr. Young, the

Reverend and any number of the men might play billiards at one another's houses or, it was rumoured, play poker, though Mrs. Greenleaf, despite her penny risks at bridge, was certain the Reverend did not participate in a game with financial stakes.

It was customary for the two women to eat in the kitchen on bridge nights. So Mrs. Young invited Mrs. Greenleaf to sit at the kitchen table while she took a white earthen ware tureen from the oven and placed it on the table between the soup bowls, bread and butter and cheese that had been laid out by Little Nettie.

Mrs. Young asked, "Would you like a glass of sherry Ivy."

"Oh dear, I don't know if I should."

"Come now Ivy, one little glass won't hurt and besides I find you play a better game when you've had a glass of sherry. It's the last of my best fino." Mrs. Young was not always quite as honest as she prided herself in being. It was her view that her friend played recklessly after two Sherries, but as she told the bridge ladies, "In love and cards you have to take every advantage you can."

Mrs. Greenleaf knew that Mrs. Young lived by this maxim when it came to bridge, and often she left the card table annoyed by her friend's play. "It is after all," she would tell her partner, "just a game." Though this thought did not trouble her when she was teamed with Mrs. Young.

Her desire to have a glass of the last of the best fino triumphed over her suspicions as to Mrs. Young's motives, and she reasoned, Mrs. Young was right, sometimes she did seem to play better after a glass of sherry. She said, "If you insist Violet."

The two friends sat and supped from the tureen of pale and delicate cream of chicken soup. Mrs. Greenleaf enjoyed the first bowl she had so much that when Mrs. Young said,

"Will you have another?" Mrs. Greenleaf happily let her fill her bowl. Then Mrs. Young said, her voice smooth like the sherry, "Would you care for another glass of fino?" Mrs. Greenleaf feeling cosseted by soup and sherry said, "Well dear, as you say it seems to help my game, and it is such a fino sherry." And she laughed at her little joke, but out of prudence added, "Of course only if you'll join me."

Mrs. Young though not half finished indulged her guest by topping up her own glass after she had filled Mrs. Greenleaf's. The autumn sky darkened in the kitchen window and Mrs. Greenleaf began to feel Mrs. Young was truly one of her dearest companions. This was a feeling she often had after drinking Mrs. Young's sherry. She reasoned it was unfair that she should deny her friend the news she had heard. Determined to be cautious she proceeded to say, "You know, my cleaning lady Greta, told me the oddest thing the other day."

"Oh really?"

"Yes, she said that she was having coffee at Beryl's house."

"Who is Beryl?"

Mrs. Greenleaf giggled, "Oh Violet, sometimes you are funny. Beryl is Little Nettie's mother."

"Oh, oh I see, that Beryl." Mrs. Young emphasized the "that" in such a way as to say that she knew many Beryls.

"Mmhm," smiled Mrs. Greenleaf, "anyway, she said that she was having coffee with Beryl and she mentioned to Beryl that she was concerned for Little Nettie."

Mrs. Young smiled to herself and said, "My dear why should she be concerned?"

Mrs. Greenleaf took another sip of the sherry and said, "Well I told her what you thought you saw." Mrs. Greenleaf stopped, realizing she had betrayed that she gossiped with her cleaning lady, so she quickly added, "I mean, after all she lives right next door to Little Nettie, in the Queen's Apartments."

"Oh is that where Little Nettie lives." Mrs. Young's lips curled into a quiet smile. "I didn't quite know that," said Mrs. Young, implying that she didn't chatter with her domestic — an implication which did not escape Mrs. Greenleaf, who sat silently. Mrs. Young apprehending that she had stopped Mrs. Greenleaf's flow, and being genuinely interested added in a coy repentant voice, "I'm sorry for cutting you off, do go on Ivy."

Mrs. Greenleaf's penchant for talking aided by the sherry prevented her annoyance from stopping her tongue. She was compelled to continue. Besides, she reasoned, Mrs. Young was not known to apologize for cutting someone off in a conversation and with the help of the sherry she decided it would be rude not to acknowledge the apology by continuing. That and the fact that she had been waiting all day to tell Mrs. Young the news.

"Thank you."

She continued, her voice conspiratorial. "Greta said she and Beryl had a bit of a cry, and Beryl confessed to her that she had been worrying about it too. Then Fred Fletcher came into the kitchen and raged, that was Greta's word, so funny too with her accent." She mimicked her cleaning lady. "If he thinks he can hit my daughter we'll take care of him." Mrs. Greenleaf chuckled. "Greta says he was watching the wrestling from Lethbridge on the TV. How those people afford a TV I don't know. But he must have been listening in. Greta said he really frightened her."

"I dare say he did," said Mrs. Young in a tone that implied she was not convinced that Greta would have been frightened. She was sure that all immigrants, particularly working class immigrants, must come from violent places and thus be accustomed to violence. Mrs. Young then said "Do you think Fred Fletcher would actually do anything?"

"I don't know what he could do really."

"Mmm, I wonder." Mrs. Young smiled and added, "If nothing else I suppose Nettie could leave him."

"But where would she go?" asked Mrs. Greenleaf.

"Couldn't she go back home? Her family would no doubt help her. Either way one does worry for her poor children!"

"Yes, those poor children," echoed Mrs. Greenleaf who had no idea what could be done, "it is too bad." The two women sat in silence, Mrs. Greenleaf finding the tragedy the greater for having finished her second glass of sherry. Mrs. Young arose from the table, gave her friend an enigmatic smile, and then said, "I shouldn't worry, these things have a way of working themselves out. I think we should await the ladies in the sitting room." She took their soup bowls and placed them in the sink. Looking out at the dark garden Violet Young wondered if Ivy Greenleaf had any understanding that she had already tipped the scales of justice. Taking her friend by the arm Mrs. Young firmly led the way into the best parlour.

It was the third Wednesday of that November when Mrs. Arthur Young and Mrs. Greenleaf met in the street in front of the Brown's Meat Market. They greeted one another by inclining their umbrellas and then Mrs. Greenleaf in a charitable tone said, "After you Violet."

"No, no, after you Ivy."

Mrs. Greenleaf anxious to get out of the rain determined

not to offer the courtesy again and walked up the stairs closing her umbrella. Mrs. Young followed suit thinking it might have been nicer of her friend to give her precedence.

Inside the store the unnatural light of the fluorescent tubes that had not been long installed heightened the dreariness of the morning by creating a brilliance of artificial white about the ladies. The brothers Brown were going about the morning tasks of cutting the meat for the display coolers.

"Morning ladies." The brothers Brown echoed one another in greeting.

"Morning, morning," said the two women shaking rain from the hems of their coats.

"What's new?" asked the dark haired brother, Bobbie.

"Oh not much," said Mrs. Young. "I'll have two and a half pounds of the ground round, please Bobbie." Turning to Mrs. Greenleaf she added, "I'm making a meat loaf for the potluck."

"That'll be nice dear. You know how everyone likes your meat loaf," purred Mrs. Greenleaf who had until that moment not been certain that her friend would attend the potluck supper. Mrs. Young could be known to be fickle about attending the potlucks as she felt that food prepared in certain homes in Fernie was not to be relied upon in matters of taste or hygiene. She also found the company to be potluck and feared having to make small talk with those she preferred to avoid. However, she had heard that Mrs. Trites Wood was going and determined that she should go to.

Mrs. Greenleaf proffered, "I'm thinking of making Lasagna."

Mrs. Young smiled at her friend. "You can never go wrong with Lasagna." It was an indulgent gesture. Mrs. Greenleaf always made Lasagna for church suppers. Eddie looked at Mrs. Greenleaf, expectation in his posture, as he waited for her order. "I'll have two pork chops, but leaner than last time, there was too much fat."

Bobbie finishing packing the ground round then said casually, "I hear that Tommie Jackson is out of the hospital now."

"Yes, he's back home," said Mrs. Greenleaf.

"No word on who punched him up? I hear that he says he doesn't know who it was. More's likely he doesn't want to remember," said Eddie.

Bobbie chuckled, "There's so many who had it in for him I'll bet they never find out who it was. Nobody'll talk."

Mrs. Young feigned disinterest. "I'll have a boiling chicken."

Mrs. Greenleaf blushed a little and then her breath coming faster said, "I hear there's a rumour that it was the Fletcher boys."

Mrs. Young raised her eyebrows. The brothers Brown both looked up and looked at Mrs. Greenleaf but said nothing.

Mrs. Young turned to her friend. "Do you mean Little Nettie's brothers."

"That's what they say."

The little bell tinkled and the four faces all turned to the door. It was Willa Carruthers. The greeting of "Morning" was saluted to the newcomer.

Mrs. Young thought Willa was not only pushy, but also a complainer who once started would not stop talking. Mrs. Young, neither wanting to hear the woman's invective nor wanting to be deterred from continuing her shopping, firmly said, "That'll be all Bobbie, please put it on my bill."

"Anything else for you Mrs. Greenleaf?" Asked Eddie.

"No, I think that's it."

The two women placed their packages into their hampers.

Mrs. Young did not speak. Mrs. Greenleaf listened with a patient smile as Willa began to pronounce that something needed to be done about the dripping faucet in the church hall. Mrs. Greenleaf said, "I'll mention it to the Reverend."

"Be sure you do," said Willa, "I've mentioned it several times and I swear the floor will rot away before it gets fixed."

"Good Day," said Mrs. Young and she opened the door of the shop. Mrs. Greenleaf followed, saying, "I'll be sure to mention it, Willa. I'll see you at the guild meeting tomorrow and we can talk more then."

Pushing up their umbrellas, Mrs. Greenleaf and Mrs. Young walked out the door and back into the rain.

Standing before the shop Mrs. Young said, "Do you think it could be the Fletcher boys who did it?"

"That's what they say. Tommie's supposed to have muttered something to the effect of, 'I'll never lay a finger on Nettie. They said they'd kill me if I did it again.'"

Mrs. Young smiled to herself. She was sure that only the Reverend could have heard what her friend was telling her, so she said, "Now Ivy, you know you can't believe everything you hear. It's probably best that we don't tell anyone this." Then she said something Mrs. Greenleaf did not understand. "Better not to have justice undone." And added something Mrs. Greenleaf did understand. "Besides, it's not like us to spread rumours." Mrs. Greenleaf nodded and the two ladies walked each their own way content to know they would meet for tea on the morrow.

THE POWER BEHIND THE THRONE

Were the Fernie of earlier times an Italian town, of say the middle ages, it might have been a mountainous Verona. A burgh of beautiful buildings, a palace of justice, churches grand and simple, and the citadels of the mercantile princes. The merchant princes in this town, like those of Verona, engaged in continual warfare but with weapons of sales and specials and price markdowns that cut and parried like sword and shield. There were several leading princes of the burgh; the battlements of their ventures larger and more impressive than all the others. The greatest of these mercantile princes was a man who in the old country might have been considered arresting but here, in this small mountain town, he was august. His accent still strongly denoted that he was not originally from here, but he was at the centre of the community. He wore a dark suit and broke his girth with a large gold watch chain. Except for the military cut of his silver hair he might have been a banker. His tenants and his employees called him "Mr. Trites Wood" and "sir". His wife knew him as Kenneth and "my dear". To his children he was "Father" or "Sir".

Mr. Trites Wood arrived at his office at 8:45 each morning. He would greet his secretary, Eileen, with a mumbled "Morning", a noise akin to clearing his throat, as she followed him into his office with a cup of tea, two lumps of sugar and one tablespoon of milk. He would sit down at his desk and Eileen would place the tea to his right and his mail and messages to his left. She would then seat herself in the chair opposite his desk and await his instructions for the morning. The particular morning in question he issued a few directives such as, "Tell Jones I want to have the Effingly figures." "Schedule an appointment with Henry. Tell him to bring the samples from Toronto." He closed with the terse words with which he always ended every interview with Eileen, "Thank you Eileen, that will be all." Eileen and her heels clicked out of the office.

Next he would look at his mail. Eileen opened all the envelopes but did not remove or disturb any of the contents. He pulled letters from envelopes, perused them quickly and made rapid scribbles in the margins placing them together with the envelopes on a pile which Eileen would later collect and work through translating the hieroglyphs into words on her Underwood Touch-Master 5 typewriter.

The morning when it all began, a taciturn grey sky had grudgingly given way to the sun, and this pleased Mr. Trites Wood. He smiled at how small the mail pile was. He would make it through the mail quickly so that he could leave early for his morning coffee. His eyes darted through each letter, his scribbles in the margin hasty and only legible to Eileen. Then he came to one particularly large manila envelope from which he extracted what looked like a map of British Columbia. It was one of those garish pieces of graphics that litter tourist information centres. The roads accurately noted, the attractions glossed over. While Mr. Trites Wood looked at the map, his usual knit brow and displeased lips began to tighten as his eyes peered ever more closely at the page. There it was, a black dot beside which was printed in black letters the word Cranbrook. Looking to the right of the black dot there was a green field of colour and then a red line which followed that series of squiggles which delineate the British Columbia — Alberta border. In the expanse of pale green that was the Rocky Mountains there was no other marker. He was sure of it, not a dot, not a speck, not a symbol, nothing, no lettering, nothing that showed Fernie. He called out, "Eileen!"

Eileen, her skirt bustling, came into the office without alarm. She was used to being called into her master's office at odd times by his strained voice. There she saw her boss, his long finger stabbing at the map set on the desk in front of him.

"Do you see Fernie anywhere on this map?" His nostrils flared. He tapped the map, "Tell me I'm wrong. Tell me Fernie is there and I'm too blind to see it."

Eileen grasped at her glasses which hung by a little silver chain around her neck and leaned over the desk. She looked at the map, pursing her lips, squinting her eyes through her bifocals at the place his finger had stabbed. "I see Cranbrook." She was certain.

"But no Fernie!"

She looked at him expectant. He looked at her satisfied. "Thank you. That will be all Eileen."

He sat at his desk looking at the map like it was soiled. His hands were on either side of the paper spread out before him but he did not touch it. He looked out his window where he could see Mount Fernie looming over the town, its snowy scalloped escarp like a leering row of teeth taunting him to set right the injustice.

He pushed away from his desk. Picking up the map between his thumb and index finger, his other three fingers splayed as though holding something they did not want to touch, he marched out of the office.

He walked through his own store and didn't notice the crooked sale sign over the arch of the women's wear department. He walked past the giggling cashiers, out the door, down the street and entered the door of the store next to his. This was the store of his tenant, the pharmacist of the town, Mr. Black. The landlord, looking like he owned the shop, not just the premises in which it was housed, walked to the back of the store to the dispensary. His gait was military, his feet stamped, and the smack of the paper of the map as it turned in his hand, caused Grandpa Williams to turn to attention despite the pain of his lumbago. He was awaiting his prescription.

Seeing who it was, Grandpa Williams greeted Mr. Trites Wood with a slight nod of the head and a "Good Morning". Grandpa, an ardent communist, sneered when greeting the capitalist class but Mr. Trites Wood did not notice him as he maintained his concentration. He merely nodded and shouted, "Morning Black." The pharmacist knew that something had annoyed his landlord, the salutation being more a bark than a word. He looked up and nodded, "I'll be just a moment Ken."

Black quickly counted the pills for Grandpa Williams and proffered the bottled relief to the Trotskyite. "Now don't be chasing after the girls again." It was Black's jocular remedy for all old men's ailments. Grandpa chuckled and hobbled away with a mumbled, "Thanks Doc."

The patient gone, Mr. Trites Wood went behind the

dispensary and, laying the map on the pill counting counter said, "Well my friend, just look at this. The Province of British Columbia has in its wisdom forgotten Fernie once again." The pharmacist peered at the map, his already ruddy face turning redder. Mr. Trites Wood smelled the familiar mixture of Old English Leather and Bourbon that always seemed to hum along with the pharmacist's breath.

Ken and George, as they were known to each other, looked at the map and saw not just a cartographer's lines and dots. They saw a dispatch from the far off capital of all things evil, namely the government in Victoria. If Vancouver was Sodom and Gomorra, Victoria was Babel. So the two of them, harrumphed, and then Black said, "It's like we don't even belong to BC."

"That's just it my friend. They don't forget us when it's time to levy taxes, but the rest of the year it's as though we aren't even a part of the province."

"Maybe we should refuse to pay our taxes." The pharmacist betrayed his ire by the purple hue that began at the tip of his reddish nose and cheeks. "Maybe we should quit the province." Black paused and then smiled somewhat shyly for someone proposing a revolution. "We could become the Republic of the Elk Valley."

Mr. Trites Wood smiled at the thought, and for a brief moment saw himself as president of the republic. But then he looked at Black more seriously. "George, that would be treason, we can't go that far. Besides I like our new flag, the maple leaf forever I say." The absurdity of the republican sentiment made them both laugh. Mr. Trites Wood, looked at his friend with a glint in his eye that Black knew indicated his landlord was mulling the problem. Then he spoke decisively, "We shall secede from British Columbia and ask Alberta to take us!"

Black did not think, he reacted. "Brilliant! Absolutely brilliant, George. We're closer to Calgary than Vancouver." Black seemed to be of the mind, like a many a citizen of the city, that Calgary was the capital of Alberta.

"And Edmonton," corrected Trites Wood. "Much closer than Vancouver, and I'll bet they'd love to have our taxes. They wouldn't forget us." Then he smiled, his teeth gritting savagely. "After this nobody'll forget us."

"But how do we do it?" asked Black, who was always keen to join a Quixotic enterprise, particularly one he had helped conceive.

Unlike his friend, Trites Wood generally preferred to avoid change, but once dedicated to a crusade he was quick to give instructions to anyone who would take the lead. "You must take it up with the Board of Trade. After all, you're president. Use your position to do some good for this town!" said the landlord, his tone final. The matter being decided, and seeing Mrs. Donnershof-Smith making her way to the pharmacy counter, he took leave of his co-conspirator.

The Board of Trade arose with indignation when Black, their president, rallied them to take action. "This egregious oversight of our fair town is the final straw. If they can forget us we shall soon forget them!" Black shouted.

The board thundered back. "Fernie shall not be forgotten!" was their hue. "We'll join Alberta!" was their cry. Though several of the more timid members were less vocal in their approval of this sedition, they kept their reservations to themselves so boisterous was the general approbation. The posturing of the apostles of foment was worthy of a painting by Jaques-Louis David, and though they might not have known that revolutionary painter, the Fernie apostles would have felt him worthy of capturing their esprit as they ran to gather that sword of the modern world — the stenographer — to whom they dictated the letters that needed to be written.

First, to that torpid pasha David Barrett, who had forgotten them, their plaint was, "Let us go!" Next they crafted their petition to the imperial Peter Lougheed of Alberta. Their plea to the imperator was simple. "Lead us out of British Columbia and deliver us from neglect." Some of the more ardent capitalists added, "From the NDP". The letter typed, it was the president, Black himself, who licked the envelope and placed the stamp upon it. Their fury spent in that final kiss of spit, the Board went out to the town and crowed over coffee at the New Diamond Grill and the Hiway Cafe of their feat of daring.

The Mayor liked to walk from his house to City Hall by a route that took him past the mountain ashes that lined the offices of the Crowsnest Coal Company. He would say to his wife when they went on an evening stroll, "I like those ashes, they're so purty." His accent proved his education for he was, as he said to his constituents, "a simple man of simple tastes." Of course, he never mentioned that the one simple confection that he enjoyed the taste of more than all others was power. This January morning as he walked past the winter stiff mountain ashes and casually allowed his eyes but not his head to turn and peer at the corner windows of the office of the man who sat in the seat of power at the Coal Company, he smiled at the thought, that though a simple man, he had joined that pantheon of princes of the town that sought to govern Fernie.

He walked across the street from the delicately frosted trees and then climbed the double set of stairs of City Hall feeling that all was as it should be on this day. He passed the offices of the administration and noted that Fred, the city clerk, greeted him with a bureaucratic smile, but the haste with which the city's clerk dropped his head back to his work betrayed something more disquieting. The mayor, not mindful of this, did notice that Miss Johnson, the secretary, had on a shorter skirt than usual. He noticed the shape of her legs as she stood up from her desk and said, "Good Morning Your Worship, I need you to sign these ordinances so that they can be posted today if possible."

He took the papers from her hands which he thought were pretty by contrast to those of his wife. Then he strode into his office leaving the door open so that he could see Miss Johnson and all other comers. Sitting down to his desk he was about to place the ordinances carefully in his "Inbox" when he saw something on the pile already there that arrested his attention. It was a cut out of a cartoon. In bold black lines he saw the fat coarse face of David Barrett, premier of British Columbia, sitting across the table from the thin aquiline aristocratic face of Peter Lougheed, premier of Alberta. The caption read, "I'll tell ya what I'll do, Pete, I'll let you have Fernie if you give us Banff." There in between the two premiers was a little voodoo doll with pins sticking from it. At first glance the mayor thought the likeness to him was remarkable, a roly-poly balding figure in a black suit. But then he thought, it can't be me, the cartoon was in the *Calgary Herald*. The cartoonist was Tom Innes, who could not know how he looked, let alone know his suit. He never wore a black suit. But he shuddered. It was a premonition, he was sure of it, the little voodoo doll portended trouble.

The mayor bellowed, "Fred!" Miss Johnson looked over to the mayor's office, eyebrows alarmed. In the mayor's tone she heard annoyance but her highly tuned political ears detected something more dangerous. Experience told her it was panic. She watched as the town administrator walked past her, his calm sashay giving him the appearance of almost floating. She had often been startled by his silent appearance over her shoulder. His long pale face entered the office of the mayor as a distended apparition of his body, and as it was his habit to walk with his hands behind his back, this posture exaggerated the vision. The mayor looked at the town administrator,

"Fred, what does this mean?" His fat fingers drummed on the newspaper.

"Well, Your Worship" — the clerk always used the formal title, as mayors might change, but administrators did not, thus he was never confused as to names — "it seems the Board of Trade has taken exception to Fernie not being on a tourism map of British Columbia."

The mayor grunted, his mind beginning to sniff around the words like they were the scent of an unfamiliar animal straying into his territory.

"Moreover, Black has whipped the Board into such a state, they've written to Premier Lougheed asking him to convert the metaphor on the map into a reality." The Clerk smiled, the curve of his lip betraying that he knew how little the mayor liked Black and that he was almost certain that the mayor would not know what a metaphor was.

"How do you mean they've written?"

"As I understand it, Your Worship, they have written a letter to the Premier of Alberta asking him to let Fernie join Alberta."

The mayor snorted, his face ruby. "What, what? Fernie, Alberta?"

The Clerk nodded at the Mayor.

The mayor spluttered. It was not that he had any particular grudge against Alberta, indeed the mayor on occasion liked very much to go shopping in Lethbridge. It was that he had heard the words Fernie and British Columbia conjoined by his grandfather from a time when he yet sat on the old man's lap sucking at a bottle. Now it felt like a bit of badly chewed apple had caught in his throat and needed to be regurgitated.

He said it again, "Fernie, Alberta!"

The Clerk stood impassive, his face only hinting at the condescension natural to a mandarin.

"I won't stand for it!"

The Clerk inclined his head, awaiting instruction.

"It won't do!"

The Clerk tilted his head. He knew that when the mayor screeched those words it was the mayor who did not know what to do.

"If I might suggest, Your Worship, perhaps you should call a press conference and advise that it is not the position of the City of Fernie that we be annexed by the Province of Alberta. You will thereby cut off the legs of this sedition and at the same time not allow your Council to waffle on the issue."

The clerk, like the mayor, had no particular aversion to the Province of Alberta, but he did have a marked dislike of change. He knew that the barrage of winds that a political change of such a magnitude might unleash would likely upset the intricate web of power he had constructed for himself.

The mayor smiled and his face became a parody of sanguine cheer. He liked the word "press conference". Mayors should hold press conferences. Besides it would give him an opportunity to tell the public that he was a little man fighting for the little man. Of course he was always disappointed when the "press conference" only amounted to the lone reporter from the *Fernie Free Press* and the young kid from CFEK Radio who covered local news when he wasn't spinning that rock and roll that the Mayor didn't like. However, they would dutifully scribble down his words and that would leave him feeling like he had accomplished something.

"Yes, yes, a press conference. That's the ticket. Arrange it for me for tomorrow." Then, with the satisfaction of knowing he had done something that day, he decided it was time to join his friends at the Fernie Meat Market to hear what the town was saying about the news.

When word got out the townsfolk began to foment and surge and bark and bustle. Letters were written, and positions declared and calls for a referendum incited and denounced.

Mr. Black often walked to his home in the Park after completing his day's work in the pharmacy. On this day, as he strolled down Main Street, he passed the Vogue cinema where he saw the playbill for a film called, "Walking Tall". He thought, that's just how I feel. It would be cantankerous not to allow him this sense of the grand, for after all, had he not signed a letter advocating that Fernie separate from British Columbia and join Alberta? Such acts of boldness had plunged entire countries into civil war and to this day blood was still shed in the name of such heresies. With these noble sentiments and the idea that he looked a bit like Joe Don Baker as sheriff cleaning up the town, he sauntered on and entered his house where he was greeted by his wife, Dolly.

Dolly was dedicated to three things in life — her children, good gossip, and being liked by everyone in town. Her children were, as they are for most mothers, paramount. Their umbilical cords having never really been severed, she lived and breathed as they did. Good gossip was her only form of entertainment and this was bound like a plait with being liked which she had had a propensity for since childhood. However, as the wife of a businessman, she felt being liked critical to the bread and butter of her children who gave her life meaning and purpose and joy. Her mission in life was keeping her husband away from that "devil drink".

Though occasionally she might gossip ill of others, Dolly was a kind soul who did not feel hatred towards anyone. The only thing she hated was alcohol. Inside a bottle of vodka or gin or rum or bourbon or any other distilled or fermented or brewed libation she saw original sin as clearly and as completely as the snake of Eve curled around an apple inside each bottle. She heard the approach of that sin each time her husband cracked open a bottle, or pulled the cork, or screwed off the cap. The pouring of that sin was the slithering of the snake into the glass.

The snake was a demon yes, but Dolly was a wily foe, worthy of the contest. She fought with every tactic and trick she had learned over her years of marriage. She knew that hiding bottles didn't work, but emptying them so that it appeared that they had been drunk from previously, leaving enough for one or two drinks, did not raise the ire of suspicion from her husband. She knew that distraction by way of food or the children was also a way to keep her husband away from the liquor cabinet. Supper was always on the table when he arrived home and they sat down to eat as soon as he washed his hands. She knew if the meal wasn't on the table he went to the liquor cabinet and took a swig of whiskey before eating.

Once he had eaten, the torpor of his contentment led him to watch the evening news or listen to the children, and this seemed to keep him away from the cabinet. Dolly never recognized two things about her husband that might have made her less a foe of alcohol. The first was that he drank to kill a pain he thought he felt, and the second was that he never drank enough to do more harm than silly words can do. Her husband was a harmless drunk and most of the time he wasn't so much drunk as he was anesthetised. Dolly loved her husband and could not see beyond his perfection. This caused her to blame others when there was question of a blemish that conflicted with her own construction of her family. She would say things like, "My George likes the odd glass, but what man doesn't drink." Then she would lean in towards her inner circle of friends as though they were conspirators and whisper with a hint of pride, "Of course when he gets together with Kenneth Trites Wood," and she would pause, "well men will be men." This was the paradoxical state she lived in: she blamed Kenneth Trites Wood for her husband's drinking but so strong was her desire to sit to the right of the throne of Mrs. Trites Wood that she accepted every invitation to the tony mansion of the doyenne of Fernie.

Dolly greeted her husband, with a smile from her thin wrinkled face that made him think of a corpse leering. George cared for his wife like he cared for any elderly woman, in a clinical way. He was repulsed by the physical being of "she" as he would call her to himself. At night he would awake and look over at his sleeping wife and wonder how he came to be married to the wrinkling dermis that contained the bones and sinew that seemed to be all he could see in her. Dolly had seen the lust in his eyes change as her body had changed after each child. As the years passed, she could not feel desire if she was not desired and so eventually she lost all drive. George did not lose his desire for sex, but he could not bring himself to have sex with her. Therefore, he drank so much that he could have sex with no one else. He struggled, for his own measure of a man was a man's ability to have sex with a woman. It was an impasse of impotence.

"George," she said, "can you please change. Remember I told you we're having supper, I mean dinner," she corrected herself, "at the Trites Woods tonight."

"Ah yes, of course. I'm looking forward to it." Dolly was surprised, for though George liked sitting down and having a drink with Kenneth he didn't like taking any meal, let alone the evening meal, at the Trites Woods. Mrs. Trites Wood served dinner, not supper, a distinction noticed in some circles but this alone was not what dismayed George about meals at the mansion. Rather he would say to his more earthy acquaintances, "That uppity bitch could suck the life out of a Lifesaver." This comment was a trifle harsh, though not completely unfounded. Mrs. Trites Wood, while a congenial hostess, could spread a chill through society by simply raising her right eyebrow.

An invitation to dinner at the mansion was something which many of the citizens of the town both longed for and feared. They accepted and then cancelled as the day came close, for the cachet of receiving the invitation was more valuable than the actual attendance. A dinner at the mansion was an affair to which only the leading citizens expected an invitation, though those who knew Mrs. Trites Wood well knew that she invited whoever she liked irrespective of their position in the town. Her dinners were tailored to meet the expectations of the guests not the hostess. The dinners most feudal in character were those to which Mrs. Trites Wood, when in a mischievous mood, invited only her very closest friends and the parvenu of the town. On such nights the guests were treated to a maid, hired for the evening, who served the food on silver platters and poured wine into cut crystal glasses.

The guests arrived according to the level of intimacy in an order which Mrs. Trites Wood herself ordained. Her closest friends were always asked to arrive slightly earlier in order to have a quiet drink before the rest. Mr. and Mrs. Arthur Young and the Reverend and Mrs. Greenleaf belonged to the former, George and Dolly to the latter. Drinks were served and though being one of the later guests, George, despite Dolly's machinations, was able to secure two vodka martinis in rather quick succession. The mayor and his wife arrived last. The mayor's wife would have liked to be early, but the mayor felt arriving last was more congruent with his station. He had delayed, forgetting first his keys and then his spectacles. This retarded the mayoral couple's arrival to such a degree that the dignity of their arrival was disrupted by the need to seat the guests as soon as possible. If there were certain things in this world, this was one of them: dinner was never served late at the mansion.

The company sat down at the long dining table. The soup, a delicate consommé, was served. George Black in an effort to open conversation with Mrs. Donnershof-Smith, the lady to his left, observed that it looked like someone had peed in the bowl. Mrs. Donnershof-Smith blushed and did not, despite a stomach that was gurgling from hunger, take another spoon of the fragrant stock. She turned her shoulder on Black and observed to Judge Dawkins, the provincial court magistrate, a man as reserved as his judgments, "My huckleberry preserves are coming to an end."

He in return said, "The flooding in West Fernie looks to have left a deal of damage for those poor citizens to clean up."

The lady nodded, and added, "Yes I shall have to get more berries next year." And so the nervous conviviality of a small town dinner where the guests know one another but do not normally socialize together soon caused the room to have that vocal buzz that is a panacea to an anxious hostess's mind. Not that Mrs. Trites Wood was ever anxious about such things.

The main course was served, a beef roast, in the English style. George Black was relieved to see a dish he could recognize. He had managed to converse with Kenneth during the soup course by shouting over the corner of the table where sat Mrs. Brummell, who had been placed to the right of Mr. Trites Wood at the head of the table. The tenant and landlord were thus separated by a lady who was only known for being the wife of the mine manager. The table seating was such that the wife of the mayor sat to Kenneth's left and next to her in unconventional fashion sat the mayor. Mrs. Trites Wood had refused to separate the mayor and his wife because she reckoned that at least they would have one another to speak with since no one in her set would be bothered to speak to them.

It was the swiftness with which the events occurred that lingered on in the minds of the dinner guests. Dolly's ears registered the sound first, though she was seated at the extreme opposite end of the table just one down from the hostess. Dolly, like the mouse which can hear pitches beyond the human ear, could hear, before the other guests, that George's voice had changed.

Dolly heard George say, "You're a gutless wonder who won't stand up to the insult that has been hurled our way."

The mayor indignant to be attacked in such a way blurted, "And you sir," he paused not sure what to say next, but then his mind formed the words that he had been thinking since the morning, "you sir, are a traitor, a traitor to British Columbia."

"Jesus Christ! You impudent fat dog, I'll horse whip ya, and anyone else who dares say I'm a traitor!"

The mayor's face turned deep purple, and he spluttered, "Are you, are you threatening me?"

"I'll punch you in the nose, right here, right now, if you dare say the word again!"

The chatter, the clinking cutlery, the laughter, all stopped and the room was quiet. Heads turned towards where the oath had come from. George Black's face had turned the colour of a red beet that had been stewed, Dolly's white face blanched so that it had the pallor of porcelain. The mayor, his lips blubbering so that he spat, "George Black, you are a traitor to British Columbia, you are a traitor to Fernie, and you are a drunk."

George Black dropped the fork in his right hand and curled the fingers into a fist. This frightened the mayor enough that he might not reason, but not so much that he was not able to react. In his hand he held the dinner roll he had been about to bite into. He curled his arm and launched the dinner roll at George Black.

The dinner roll reached high speed as it flew across the table but its aim was not true. The roll arced towards Mrs. Donnershof-Smith, grazed her rouged cheek and became stuck in the florid curls of gold that hung from the elderly matron's ear. The ball of bread pulled on her earring and Mrs. Donnershof-Smith yelped as the earring and roll became entangled in her coiffure. The force of the roll and the pain of the tearing of the lobe caused the portly lady to lose her equilibrium. She tipped from the side of her chair. In an effort to steady herself her robust arm flailed and her heavily bejewelled hand caught the gilt edge of her dinner plate causing it to act as a catapult. The food she had not yet eaten rose into the air and somersaulted into the lap of George Black.

The mayor rejoiced as he saw retribution come in the way of the dry beef and drippings. His glee was shortened by the sharp jab of his wife's elbow which hit his ribs squarely so that he jerked his head in time to see the befuddled Mrs. Donnershof-Smith lift her coiffure and then her head up from the judge's lap where her hair and head had come to rest as she tipped sideways.

The mayor spluttered.

The mayor's wife said, "Oh dear, oh dear, are you alright?"

Mrs. Donnershof-Smith was being righted by the judge who blushed and did not know where to turn his face.

"Apologize you great oaf," the wife of the mayor shouted at her husband.

The mayor recognizing the gravity of the moment spluttered, "I am, am sorrrry my my lady."

Mrs. Trites Wood turned her head from the Reverend with whom she had been conversing, trying to ignore the fracas at her husband's end of the table. The little wrinkles about her eyes and lips remained stolid, but the colour of her eyes changed from the merry blue of a hostess to grey disdain and then to wicked amusement as she looked down the long table first at Dolly, then the mayor's wife, the mayor, her husband, and finally to the face of George Black.

"Excuse me Reverend." She rose and made her way to Mrs. Donnershof-Smith. She approached the woman who was being helped from her chair by the judge.

"My dear Mrs. Smith." Mrs. Trites Wood refused to use the double-barrelled name that the woman had herself created. As she led the victim of the assault towards the powder room she turned her penetrating eyes to her husband. He nodded assent.

Mr. Trites Wood rose. "George old man, perhaps you'd better come with me."

George had been so engrossed in the sequence of events that had followed the bunning of the beehive (Mrs.

Donnershof-Smith's signature hair) that he had failed to note the trajectory of the beef. As he stood up the roast beef, gravy and potatoes began to slide off his lap. He clutched at his crotch and brought up a collage of meat, gravy and potato which he placed on his plate with a care that suggested he might eat them. As he rose he turned to the Mayor, smiled and said, "As you all can see, our Mayor can't even throw a bun, let alone run this town!" Bowing to the assembly he turned to his wife and said, "C'mon Dolly let's go." Then, turning to his friend, "Ken tell your little missus we appreciate her fine hospitality, but we won't be insulted by the likes of that two bit political hack."

"C'mon Dolly, now!"

Dolly rose, the white of her face splotched with colour as though blood had been spilled on flour. Her eyes watered. She was both humiliated and enraged that the Mayor should dare to insult her husband and that she should be forced to walk out of a dinner party at the mansion. But she knew no alternative. Her husband had spoken and it would be disloyal and a great breach of protocol not to depart. Besides she was getting a migraine, something which often occurred when her husband was in society.

Kenneth walked with them into the foyer. As he opened the door he said, "Good on you George! You can be proud of your husband Dolly." Dolly grimaced, but for his power over them she would have told him off. How dare this man ply her husband with drink and then escort them to the door in disgrace with such jovial cheer?

The other dinner guests bid one another goodbye shortly after the dessert had been served. Never had a party at the mansion come to an end so quickly. The couples walked their way home, or got into their automobile, chattering nervously about the events of the evening. The spiteful were filled with glee at the thought of the chat they would have with friends about the scene at the Trites Wood's dinner. The politically astute concentrated on the altercation between the Mayor and George Black.

After saying good bye to the guests, the hosts returned to the sitting room where coffee had been hastily served. There Kenneth poured himself a scotch and Mrs. Trites Wood sipped a bit of cold coffee. They sat silently looking at the embers in the grate of the fire place. Then Mrs. Trites Wood rose, straightened her pearls, looked over at her husband and said as she walked out of the room, "It won't do Kenneth." Her husband nodded.

The next day, in the morning, after finishing his mail, Kenneth Trites Wood made his way through his premises stopping to admonish the little stock boy. "Carter," he bawled, "in my establishment we tuck our shirts in to our trousers. None of your slacking about here lad." Then he continued on past the cashiers and cast a glance that caused Nancy to put her painted fingernails which she had been admiring under the counter where they could not be seen. He continued on to the door of the pharmacy where he saw Dolly. He greeted her with a tone that made her feel she had been caught doing something untoward. She quickly folded up the *Fernie Free Press* she had been reading to glean how her husband faired in the battleground of public opinion.

Kenneth walked to the back of the store where George was chatting with the new pretty secretary from the radio station. Kenneth greeted her stonily. He did not care for the mini-skirts the young women were beginning to wear in Fernie. Turning to his friend he said, "George, old man."

"Ken."

"I need to have a word, in private."

"Why don't we go into the stock room?"

"Yes, yes, that's a good place."

George led the way down the stairs and into the basement stock room where a small wooden table and several chairs were set out for the staff coffee breaks.

"Have a seat." George pointed to one of the chairs, but before seating himself he opened a box and removed two shot glasses and a bottle of bourbon. George filled each shot glass and then sat down.

Kenneth did not like Bourbon. He found it too fragrant a drink. He preferred scotch, but he obliged his friend. George raised his glass, Kenneth did likewise and they downed their shots.

"George, I think we've got to let this Alberta thing go."

"What, what d' ya mean, let it go."

"Well George, I just think it might be better if we let this one go."

George's hand shook as he picked up the bottle and leaned towards Kenneth's glass.

"No, no thanks." Kenneth put his hand over the shot glass. George slowly poured himself another and swished it on his palate.

The glorious revolution was quelled. The only injury, beyond embarrassment, was to Mrs. Donnershof Smith's ear and coiffure. Black and the mayor huffed and puffed back and forth for a time, but without conviction. The tempest raged longer than it might have because a few others who were not so great but who liked to see their name in the press wrote letters of protest for a month or so. The imperator Lougheed sent a kindly letter. Barrett deigned to not. The lofty *Globe* picked up the story as did some of the other papers, though none could know that the matter had been settled in a quiet fashion.

The revolutionaries enjoyed many more years of

bourbon and scotch and comforted themselves with the satisfaction of never seeing another tourism map without a black dot and the word Fernie more or less loosely placed in the right hand corner that contained the toe of British Columbia.

LAID TO REST

Grief is a boxer on a hot sunny afternoon, no breeze, sky blue, no clouds. Jab, Sucker, Jab. One of our beloved citizens has died and the town is gathering in mourning. No church is big enough and we meet at the Fernie Community Centre. I have often thought the name is ugly, but that it suits the building which by some twist of comedic architectural hideousness is a tin shack of large proportions. Were it mere corrugated tin it might not be so bad, but this tin shack is one of those monstrosities sprayed in a 1970's colour. It is dirty blue and what might be called mustard yellow, though wise-guy teenagers have a more earthy description. As if the structure knows this, it sits ashamed, its roof hunched over against the beauty of the mountains and town around it.

Inside it is no better. There is no charm or grace to redeem the exterior. It is a big empty hall, with walls of paneled wood and with a raised stage at one end. To this refectory of noxious ambiance, the mourners arrive, girding themselves, if they have the least bit of taste. Perhaps they are the lucky ones, the less aesthetic. They drive up in their cars and curse if they have come too late and cannot find parking in the parking lot. Just across the street there is vacant space. However, it offends their right of proprietorship in the Community Centre if they have to park anywhere but in front of the door. Or, if they come walking, while not being distracted by a want of parking, they notice how tight their trousers have become.

It is a truth of small town life that clothes are either "comfortable but ugly or ill-fitting and out of style". However, no clothes are more ill-fitting than the suit saved for special occasions. This item of clothing is often the most reviled of the wardrobe. Seldom worn, it is frequently the one purchased for a groom's wedding and often lasts until his own funeral. Being from the rack and badly tailored, the suit does not fit on the day of the wedding. It is bought slightly too big, the wearer conscious that he will wear it again when he is not quite so youthfully proportioned. In its early days this suit is worn to the odd wedding of a friend who importunes the wearer by having a more formal affair. Each time he hears of a wedding the wearer hopes the bride will allow casual attire. In later years the suit is worn more often to funerals than to weddings and such is the case on this day.

Women are not spared from this sartorial plight. There is the going-to-funeral black polyester suit consisting of an ill-fitting jacket, usually too big, with a plain black skirt, all the biases inaccurately sown, and the hem, not so much uneven as it shows the tug of the stitch. The whole hides a blouse of white polyester. The ensemble sits on sturdy legs with feet reposing in either comfortable flat shoes of the wrong colour or a pair of strapped sandals in a shiny plastic white or black.

The lesser or more casually inclined citizens come

without suits and one sees ill-fitting trousers and shirts of every colour. Those who care about how they look appear in the clothes of a good tailor or in the latest fashions from the very best shops in Calgary, Vancouver or Spokane. They carry labels of Holt Renfrew and Henry Singer prominent in the linings of these guises of the rich or stylish. Like the less well-dressed they too sweat in the heat, but they either sit smugly thinking of how much better they look than the rest of us, or more likely, glance distractedly at their watches wondering why the event hasn't started as indicated on the black rimmed card affixed to the notice board next to the library.

The hall is filled to capacity. At the wake everyone will say there was standing room only, and that means there must have been somewhere around five hundred mourners. For such large numbers to gather, everyone knows that the person in the casket must have been of great importance. The mourners, aware that it would be untoward and disrespectful to make a noise, speak quietly but there are so many that the hall reverberates with hushed whispers broken by the squeal of chairs on the wooden floor as someone slides the plastic glides against the lacquer to get a better view. Since most everyone knows everyone else they must either greet, or avoid one another, as the circumstances of their relationships require. As they come into the hall, they sneak peeks to ensure that they move towards those who will welcome them and away from those who might not return a nod or smile. There are of course those who are either oblivious to the various enmities, calumnies or jealousies of the town; or, refuse to admit them because of position or need. Those involved in local politics greet everyone. In stark contrast, members of the "big families" neither greet effusively nor avoid anyone. They are firm in their purpose to find a seat suited to them and hope to rise above the town gossip, the innuendo and the squabbles.

I sit and watch as the family of the deceased march in to the dirge of the bag pipes. Each of the dead man's relatives, lost in their grief, stifles sniffles. The widow leans into her son's strong arm that must act as a crutch; her grey hair is a light bouffant coifed and sprayed as stiffly as she hopes her back appears to the onlookers.

The man who has died was unusual, not because he was a doctor, rather because he was the town doctor. Our doctor. My doctor. For decades he tied umbilical cords, mended limbs, counseled hot flashes, declared lumbago, cleared the clap, abraided impotence, and finally pronounced for many, but not himself, that the last breath had been taken. He is the last of this breed that Fernie will see, that likely any of us will ever see. Things are different in the world now: we can choose from among a number of doctors but we cannot pay them with a chicken.

The bagpiper finishes and his bags sputter then wheeze. I turn my attention from the bier to the others in the hall. I see the service will be ecumenical: the priest, the pastor, the deacon — the full compliment of clergy is here. The youth groups the doctor supported are represented by boys from the Cadets and the local hockey team; they stand awkwardly shifting from foot to foot. I look down the aisle and across to the row on the other side of me and there I see her.

She is in my row, across the aisle, two seats down. She looks like she did before, long ago. Her long blonde hair carefully curls on each side of her head like a drape opening to reveal her round full face. From where I sit she does not look much changed, perhaps a little heavier, a droop at the jaw line, eyebrows not as arced. She sees me too. She gives a thin smile. Her lips never were full, but time has made them menacing. She is wearing an elegant black suit, almost Chanel. She used to wear pastel pink, yellow and blue when she walked into the school, sometimes in a twin set with a deep V that taunted us boys to look at her bosom. I remember the first time she spoke to me; she caught me eyeing her famous (at least to the boys in Fernie High) breasts and she said, "You like what you see?" Though seventeen, she was already used to boys like me looking at her; after all she was a big city girl. I could tell she knew how to handle a wolf whistle.

I'm fairly sure I blushed.

"You don't like what you see?"

I nodded trying to look worldly.

"Can't you talk?"

"Uh huh."

"That it?"

"No."

She laughed, her breasts shook, in a way that I learned meant she was happy. And I learned she was never happier than when she embarrassed a boy.

"Why don't you take me for coffee?" She asked in a way that I knew was not a question but a command. I hesitated thinking about what acerbic Mrs. Norris would say if I cut class, but I knew even her stinging rebuke would be worth it.

We went to the Hiway Café on the edge of town where the east bridge crosses the Elk River. It was a roadside diner in a log cabin. The waitress, who smelled strongly of scent, poured weak coffee into the mugs on the table and told anyone who wanted to know what the perfume was: "Why a little 'Evening in Paris' my Barry gave me."

She asked us, "Yous all want some pie with your coffee? Beryl's made it fresh." We stuck with the coffee. The waitress, whose name was Verna and who had been working in the coffee shop for over twenty years, till something better came along, gave me a wink. I blushed again.

She asked, "Do you always blush so much?"

I told her I did.

What was the point of lying, I always blushed when a woman looked at me. I told myself it was probably hormones, but it was really that I was afraid every woman could tell what I was thinking. Didn't every boy betray lustful thoughts as easily as I did?

"I like it," she said taking a sip of her coffee.

I blushed again. I tried to calm myself by sucking some coffee into my mouth.

As I set down my cup she took my hand.

"I'll bet you've never kissed a girl, have you?"

I stopped breathing. If I inhaled I'd choke on the coffee, if I exhaled I'd spit it all over her.

Her breasts jiggled. She was really happy. I felt like I was turning blue. I dropped her hand and stood up tipping my chair over. I ran out the door and into the parking lot where in a jagged gasp I spat out the coffee; it was absorbed by the Indian Summer dust of the dirt. I wanted to be absorbed by the dust, too. But I went back into the café where everyone was looking at me.

"You all right? Anything wrong with the coffee?" asked Verna, her tone snide, and then she laughed as did the other patrons.

She shot a bitch look at Verna and then she looked at me, real concern in her eyes. "Really are you alright?"

I shrugged, mortification removing my last pride. I couldn't say a word.

"Let's get out of here," she commanded again, throwing a fresh green dollar bill on the table; the Queen's face up.

She took my hand and we walked along the edge of the

highway up to the bridge; its girder's rusting, looking like a derelict derrick tipped over the water. We stood on the edge of the bridge leaning against the wooden railing. She tilted her head over the rail and spat into the river, the white bubbles twirled and disappeared into the swirling water as it swept under the bridge.

"Now you do it." Her eyes excited. I filled my mouth with saliva and tried to spit, lots and far.

"Make a wish!" she shouted, laughing as the wet mass arced and landed on the water, its bubbles floating under the bridge before they ebbed into the current.

"Don't tell me what you wished for." I didn't.

She grabbed my hand and led me back to her car, a little black Mustang. I didn't own a car. I felt uncool, it was wrong for a boy to let a girl drive, but I had no choice. My family couldn't afford more than a used four-door. I learned to drive in a deep blue Pontiac Parisienne. Her car made me feel sexy, even in the passenger seat. We drove back to school and she told me about Vancouver, which she missed. She had had to move to Fernie because her dad had got one of the big jobs with the mine. He was an executive. I didn't tell her I was a miner's son, at least not then. At school I got out of the car and walked around to open her door. She howled with laughter. I was glad, it kept her breasts jiggling.

My Don Juan move must have pleased her, or so I thought. She said, "Meet me after school by the car." She was confident in her power over me. Usually, after class, I went to work at the Dixie Lee chicken stand down on the highway, but I knew I'd be late and go meet her.

I couldn't wait for school to be over. I hastened to the car. She came a few minutes later, talking to some of her girlfriends. She threw me the keys.

"Drive."

I unlocked the passenger door; her girlfriends got in the back. I got into the driver's seat. She sat next to me.

"Where to?" I looked at the dashboard trying to be nonchalant.

"Let's go cruising."

We joined the procession of cars that drove up and down Main Street after school. It was a circuit that everyone with a car and with no job to go to did after school. Even the adults did it; we thought it was about the most interesting thing to do in town, unless there was a good film at the Vogue Theatre or a bush party.

I listened to the three girls chattering and I was just happy to be inside a car cruising up and down Main Street. I felt important. I felt good.

We dropped off the girls and then she said, "Take me home."

We drove to her house in silence. I stopped the car; she leaned over and took my head in her hands and kissed me. Her tongue pushed my lips open. Our spit mingled; this time I was slobbering wet like the river. She bit my lip hard so that it stung. I yelped and she laughed.

I got out of the car and ran to Dixie Lee. I was late for work; it wouldn't be the last time that autumn.

Every couple of days or so, she asked me to drive and then we cruised; sometimes with her friends, sometimes without. The first snows started to fall, the roads got icy, but we still cruised, CFEK blaring on the radio, car windows foggy from our breath and damp jackets. Then one day she said she'd pick me up from work. Her parents were out of town. Why didn't I come over, we'd mess around. I said sure.

And we did mess around. By then I was an old pro at kissing and we sat on the sofa in front of the TV necking. The Brady Bunch muffled the smooch of our kisses that tasted of stale cigarettes and vodka and coke which she had poured and we shared. Sometimes my mind wandered and I thought of Marcia and then I thought how much she looked like the Brady girl and everything felt ok.

Suddenly, we were past petting. Our clothes came off, blouse, bra, trousers, shirt. I was not thinking much, I was feeling everything in a way I'd never felt before. My skin voltaic in contact with hers. I was "hornier 'an hell," as the boys said, bragging in the locker room. I coursed her body with my hands, cheeks, lips, tongue. She moaned and whispered, "I want you in me."

I almost choked on her breast, but I pulled down my underpants. I fumbled as I tried to slip hers down; she seemed to know what to do. I was a virgin; I guessed she was not. I was surprised to be on third base already.

She led me in. It didn't quite feel like the boys had told me it would but she helped to bring me home. She yelped so that it hurt my ear, "Pull out before you come." I tried.

"Christ!!" she swore, "you fucking idiot, I told you to pull out before you came."

"I tried," I said, my voice, my penis, my ego, suddenly limp.

"Get the fuck out of here," she was yelling, her voice panicky, "I gotta clean up." I didn't know what this meant, but I pulled up my underpants and trousers, buttoning my shirt as I ran to the foyer. Pushing on my sneakers I dashed out into the cold, clear night forgetting to close the door. I ran past the big houses in the Park. I ran down Main Street the shop windows mirroring my distress back at me. I ran all the way home, slipped past my parents and quietly crept into my room where I didn't sleep all night.

She saw me the next day in school. "Sorry about last night."

"Me too. I didn't know it would happen so fast." I choked on the words. I was so embarrassed.

She laughed, but her breasts didn't jiggle. "Well, let's hope those critters of yours don't swim too fast. I cleaned up as best I could." I began to understand.

It wasn't too long after that I found out my critters could swim fast, real fast. It was December when she told me she was pregnant. She did it kindly, sort of.

Remember your little accident?" I couldn't think of what she was alluding to.

"You know, as ye sow, so shall ye reap." I looked at her, not comprehending, though the first inkling must have been taking root in my mind.

"Look bozo, how much more blunt do I need to be?" Despite her sour tone she was savouring my naiveté.

"I'm pregnant."

My stomach slammed against my heart.

"Oh my God!" was what I said.

I repeated it over and over: "Oh my God! Oh my God!" like somehow He was going to help us if I said it often enough.

"Promise me you won't tell anyone." Was she joking! Like I was going to tell anyone. I felt like running away from town, from this.

I became conscious of a shrill edge to her voice, the quiver of panic. She was scared too. I kept hearing the words "Oh my God" over and over in my head. It was like the whirring of a flywheel with a broken cog. I realized I had to say something intelligent, adult. I wished I were still a kid, but I had to be mature. Shit, I thought, I didn't even make it beyond a few strokes; I hardly had time to feel anything and already I was going to be a father. I was only sixteen. I didn't want to be selfish, but that was how I felt. I didn't want to be a father.

She looked at me with a mixture of contempt, revulsion and terror, her face ugly. I wondered what I saw in it, and then I remembered, it wasn't her face. I looked at her breasts. I saw a little boy, my son, suckling them. Something I'd done and I'd never do again. I didn't know for sure, but I felt it, her face told me it.

The only thing I could think to ask, "Do your parents know?"

She laughed bitterly and then she slapped me, hard, so that my cheek stung and my jaw hurt for a couple of days.

"That's what my dad said; my mom just asked how a daughter of hers could be such a slut."

"I'm sorry," I said, suspecting it was not the right thing to say, but it was how I felt and it was all I could think of.

Tentatively I reached for her hand. "Do they know I'm the dad?"

"Are you kidding? I can't tell them it was you; they'd even be more upset. Christ. Plus, my dad'd get your dad fired."

We stared at each other, the silence embarrassing me. I had to say something, so I offered, "We could get married."

She looked at me like I'd lost my mind.

For the first time I realized that she was embarrassed because I was a coal miner's son, not good enough even to be the father to our bastard. And I was in her power. Her father controlled my family's destiny.

She started to laugh, a deep patronizing laughter. "No," she said, "that's very noble of you, but I think I'll manage on my own." She turned away from me and got into her little black sports car and drove off leaving me standing in the cold grey afternoon; and like in every teen romance cliché movie at the Vogue snowflakes started to fall. The difference was that I was living the cliché and it didn't seem so obviously cliché to me.

That was the last time I saw her. Until today. Rumour had it that her parents sent her to boarding school because she was getting in with the wrong crowd. I kept thinking she was sent away to have the baby and would be back after; and a barren woman, sometimes the grandmother, would have a new unexpected baby. There were darker rumours, but mostly that was how it was done in those days in Fernie. She never came back.

Now I see her sitting across the aisle from me her face looking intently at the eulogists. I keep glancing sideways to see her. She doesn't look at me, not once throughout the whole funeral. She sits, her back straight, her legs crossed at the ankles, her hands folded into her lap. As the ceremony comes to an end I assume that we will walk down the aisle together, if I time my exit from my chair. She will have to face me. But as I stand the person in the chair behind me taps my shoulder so that I have to turn back. Standing behind me is one of my clients, a thin frail old man the doctor used to play bridge with every Thursday. He was the town Vet until his osteoarthritis made handling animals too difficult. He leans in to me and says, "He'd be pleased to know that you came. He always held you in high regard." I wonder why and as though hearing me the Vet says, "He liked it that you pulled yourself out of the mine, by your own two boot straps as it were."

"Oh." I'm not sure what to say when someone says something like that. My father was a proud miner and I am not ashamed to say I am his son. But the Vet is old Fernie and I know he means it as a compliment so I just say, "I'm sure you'll miss him." The Vet sighs, shakes his head, "There aren't too many of us left, are there?" I know, too, he means "old-timers".

"No, I suppose not." I change my face so that it looks

like what I hope is suitably wistful. I look around for her but she is gone. I walk out with the Vet, disappointed not to talk to her but hopeful she'll come to the tea after the interment. All the way down the aisle and to the door I am greeted by familiar faces, faces that have grown old in Fernie. There are few fresh faces and I wonder if the Vet isn't right.

I look for her outside the community centre. She is not in the little circles of people who stand together in clusters as they try to shift sweat clinging underclothes away from their skin; some catching up on news and gossip of neighbours they only see at weddings and funerals; some talking of the doctor; others wondering what they'll be served at the tea. I see her standing alone in the shade cast by the building, the elegance of the cut of her suit heightened by the crude corrugation of the centre walls behind her. I wonder if she has been waiting for me to come out. She has lit a cigarette; the smoke idly plays around the tip in the breezeless afternoon. She smiles as I approach. Not necessarily a welcoming smile. It might be the smile she gives a doorman.

"Hi." She exhales smoke, and holds out her hand. I shake it lightly, the way it is proffered.

"Hello"

"You look good," she says, "time has been kind to you." Her tone is genuine.

"You too." This time she smiles wryly. She is used to being complimented, but disingenuously.

"Would you like a cigarette?" she takes a pull at hers.

"No, I quit years ago."

"Smart, no wonder you look so good. Your wife ought to be careful though, bet all the girls in town still chase you."

"No wife," I say feeling like it's not the answer wanted. I could still marry but don't think it likely.

"You?"

"Me? No, no wife." She laughs amused by her own joke, I kind of smile, and then she adds, "but I do have a husband."

"Good."

"I wouldn't say that," she says, "he's not good, but he's ok and he keeps me in the style I like and that's worth something too."

My stomach flutters. I ask with as composed a tone as possible, "Kids?"

Her face softens, "Yeah, even a grandchild." She pauses, "What about you?"

"No, none." I don't know what to feel about what she and I have just said.

Her gaze doesn't break from mine. I feel like she's going to tell me about her kids. I want to ask, "Is one of them mine?" But I can't. I hope she'll say something. She doesn't though; she just looks across the parking lot, through the shimmer of heat waves rising from the hot asphalt. She looks up to the mountains.

To break the silence I ask, "So what brings you to the funeral?"

She puts the cigarette up to her lips. Lines of discontent tighten around her slightly tired, brownish-red lipstick-smudged lips as she pulls in the smoke. She looks at the Three Sisters as she exhales.

"I always hated those mountains, that bloody frown, like they always disapproved of me."

Between us there is the silence of strangers who have seen one another's privates, yet know nothing about each other. Were it not for the mourners breaking up to go to the cemetery or the tea there would be a complete stillness.

She finally breaks the silence, her voice dry. "The good doctor gave me the best piece of advice I ever got in my life."

Then she adds, "I couldn't believe he was dead when I heard it. I just thought I'd come to pay my respects."

"Oh?" I can't quite read her tone.

"I see you're still the conversationalist you were." She chuckles, and not bothering to hide the contempt says, "I suppose you're up at the mine?"

It's my turn to laugh, "No, I'm a lawyer." She raises her right eyebrow, and I go in for the punch, "I suppose you're still a spoiled rich girl."

She laughs, then purses her lips around the cigarette, sucks on it, and from amidst the smoke expelled as though she were blowing out a candle says, "I've paid my dues." She exhales the last smoke and throws the butt onto the ground crushing it into the asphalt with her patent black pumps.

I want to scream at her, "What happened to our child?" but I'm silent, not sure if I'm afraid of her reaction to the question. Or is it, that I'm afraid of the answer.

She looks at me and then glances at a black Mercedes that is pulling up next to us.

"That's me." She leans in towards me.

"It's been nice to see you." She kisses my cheek, and turning, walks towards the idling car that waits for her. She looks back one last time. Is there a tear on her cheek? She gets into the car, the door closes, and slowly it drives away. The smell of cigarette smoke and her skin lingers. It might have been forty years ago but she still smells the same.

I look at the remaining mourners who watch the last of the funeral cortege leave; the body is going up the hill to the cemetery. They shuffle about, relieved to be taking off suit jackets, loosening ties, wiping sweat, adjusting suspenders, fanning faces, shifting girdles, dropping a high heel. I wonder how many are glad their secrets are going into the grave with the good old town doc.

SURVIVAL OF THE FITTEST

Wally hated shopping. It was not the shopping itself which was so hateful, it was his sure knowledge that a man didn't do the shopping. Not a real man anyway. Shopping was woman's work, or kids chores, but a man, he didn't shop. Of course, Wally didn't have a woman to do the shopping. He was a bachelor, so every week on his day off he would go to the Overwaitea store, as early as he could so that no one would see him and he would do his shopping. He would move around the aisles of the store quickly not looking at anyone in case they might recognize him. He used to go to the MC Cash Grocery and the odd time he went to the Trites Wood store when they still sold groceries, now he mostly confined himself to the Overwaitea store. It wasn't too far from where he lived and the cashiers would flirt with him. Not with any seriousness though; after all, Wally wasn't a serious catch. He didn't have a job at the mine like the other men; he used to shovel coal into the boilers in the basement of the Trites Wood building until they installed new fangled gas boilers, then he was out of a job. After that he was a stock boy, but that didn't last too long and he drifted from odd job to odd job, until after the winter of the year that he and Billy went fishing one last time. Then he got a job with the City clearing snow in the winter and mowing lawns in the summer and picking up garbage when one of the men on the truck was sick or on holidays. But now Wally was more vagrant than settled.

Wally had a best friend, or at least that's what Wally told himself he had. His best friend was Billy. It was Billy's fault that Wally hated shopping. Billy never went shopping. Billy had married straight out of high school, his high school sweetheart. It had been clear to Billy from sometime after his sixteenth birthday that if he didn't find a wife when high school was over he'd be in trouble. That was because his mother said, "Boy the day you graduate from high school is the day you're on your own. I ain't cookin' and cleanin' for you anymore. An' another thing, you're gonna pay rent if you plan on stayin' here."

Billy's father just said, "Listen to your mother, you know she means business." Billy's father had been listening to his wife since before they had married. One of, if not the greatest ambition Billy had, was to escape his mother. So even before he graduated, he applied for a position at the mine, and the day after the last day of school he started to work. By the end of the summer he was married. Billy married a meek little thing who was a perfect bride for a man such as Billy. She didn't say much and she looked after the house and so long as Billy came to dinner on time and took off his boots before he came into the house she didn't nag — too much.

Billy, having established himself in life, was able to rib his friend Wally. "See you bin out doin' the shoppin'. My misses, she does that. She does the cookin' too! Why don't you come over for supper tomorrow for a square meal?" And Wally would nod his head and look forward to the next night when he wouldn't have to open a tin and heat it up. He looked forward to a properly cooked meal. For what Billy's wife lacked in conversation she made up for in her cooking skills.

Billy felt it was his job to bring home his pay check so that, "my misses can buy the grub." But Billy was prepared to boast that he could bring home the "grub" if such was caught from a stream or shot by a rifle. One day, even though it was late autumn and the fishing might not be good, Billy thought he should cast his rod one last time before the snow fell.

Billy stopped his pickup in front of Wally's house and tooted the horn. Wally lived in the Annex neighbourhood where he rented a little basement suite from the McAllister family. The family lived upstairs with four sniveling brats and another on the way. Wally lived downstairs. The basement suite was two rooms. One was a little bedroom with a toilet and washstand. The other had a sink and hot plate, which Wally described as "the kitchen". When he walked exactly two paces to the table and three chairs he claimed to be "in the dining room". And when he leaned one of the dining chairs against the wall of the room, he called this area "the living room". Wally was happy to have his own space. It was much better than living with his mother who'd taken to drinking and shouting praise and exaltation to the Lord in church and at home after the death of his father in a logging accident.

Wally, who'd been waiting for Billy to toot his horn, ran out his door and up the basement steps. In one hand was his fishing rod and tackle box, in the other hand a crumpled brown bag, his lunch. He placed the rod and tackle box next to the case of beer in the back of the truck, opened the door and climbed in. As he got in he noticed the gun rack was carrying Billy's rod on the top rack and on the two hooks set below the fishing rod was a rifle.

Wally placed his lunch bag on the seat next to his lap.

"You figure you're not gonna catch any fish?" Billy was counting on a fish being his lunch. His cast iron pan was under the seat.

"Nah, but you know I like a little' something to go with my fish. I brung us some peanut butter an' jam san'wiches."

"You're a sick bastard."

"What? It's real good, you gotta try it."

They drove away from Fernie on the highway for a short while and then out onto the logging road that led up into the Bull River territory. The dirt road was hard and dry but rutted from the rains of September. Hunting season was over and seeing no loggers about Billy drove as fast as he could, gripping the steering wheel tightly so that the truck could move along at a pace that left a billow of dust behind. Wally held on to the bench of the seat so he didn't get jostled off it. He wanted to say "slow down" to Billy, but he knew he'd get teased if he did, so he sat quietly trying not to let his tongue get in the way of his clattering jaw.

The truck rattled on until they came to a break that Billy spotted in the bush. Slowing down, he turned into a soft grassy track, an overgrown old logging road that ran up to the edge of meadow. Billy stopped the truck and got out. He leaned in and took out his rod and said, "Wally bring us a beer." Wally opened his creel and stuffed a couple of beers in it. Then slinging his waders over his shoulder and taking his tackle and rod followed Billy across the meadow towards the river. The grass of the meadow was dull brown and gold, and the heads of the grass seed hung low, bending back towards the ground. The thistles had mostly gone to seed and the heads looked like bedraggled old ladies whose hair had not been set and whose teeth were not in. The burrs looked for the edges of Billy and Wally's trousers and stuck to them so that the men had to pick them off once they got to the river's edge.

It was a still day but for noise made by a couple of thickly furred squirrels out gathering seeds, chattering with annoyance at the men for entering their territory. High over them a lone eagle glided eyeing the squirrels. The men sat on the bank of the river drinking a beer as they set up their tackle and lures and each arranged his rod to his liking. Then they put on their waders and walked out into the river casting as they went. After a time Wally caught a fish and placed it in his creel.

Billy cast for a while but then he got bored. He went back to the truck and came back with a wire. He made a snare and gently placed it into the pool upstream of the fish he could see there. He let it float down stream as though it were a twig slowly meandering past the fish. Carefully he moved the wire snare up past the fish's head and gills, then with a quick flick of his hands he captured the fish around its body and flipped it out of the water. He hooted with glee, ran up onto the bank and hit the fish on its head with his fish paddle made from the cut off end of an old broom. He put the fish on the bank of the river. Billy smiled with delight. He preferred snaring fish to catching them with a rod. It was quicker and he didn't have to fiddle with the hook.

Before long Billy had eight fish lying on the bank. Wally still had only caught the one. Billy went back to the pick-up, reached into the box and pulled a beer out. He looked at the label for a moment. Then, using his belt buckle, he flipped the cap off the stub brown bottle. Though autumn was cool, the bottle was not as cold as he would have liked it to be. He asked himself why he didn't think to put it in the creek. He guzzled the bottle dry and opened another. This bottle he drank more by sips as he leaned against the cab of the pick-up in the wan sun and looked across the meadow. He made a careful study of the trees. It was then that he noticed the elk. It was a big one. He whistled under his breath, "whoo wee". He watched the animal as its head went up and down feeding in the tall grasses where the forest and the meadow met.

For a time Billy watched the animal, its mien proud even as its snout pulled at the blades of grass and chewed them. As slowly and as quietly as possible he turned into the truck cab and pulled the gun from the rack. He undid the safety and lifted the gun to his chest. He looked down the top of the barrel, aligned the elk in the sight and he pulled the trigger. There was a loud bang. The animal looked up as Billy pulled the trigger again. The elk stood as though held in the air by its horns. Billy wondered if he had missed. Then the elk cambered slightly away from Billy before falling to its side. Even in this motion it was regal, as though the animal knew it had to die in a stately way.

The bull lay, the hulk of its torso a smooth curve of tawny brown against the blades of the deep grass, its horns twisting the head so that its eyes faced the sky. It was a big one. Billy didn't think he'd ever seen such a big one before. He put the gun onto the seat of the truck. Then he picked up his beer and walked over to the elk.

Wally came running. He'd heard the shots from the meadow and had waded up the river bed and across the rocks of the bank as fast as he could. There he saw Billy standing with a beer bottle in his hand, his right foot on the back of the elk, his face a grin of triumph.

Wally put down his rod and sauntered over to Billy who now was sitting on the mound of the elk.

"Look what I got me." Billy patted the elk's fur.

"What the hell. Why'd you shoot it?"

"Christ it'll keep us in meat all winter, Wally."

"Billy it's not huntin' season. What we gonna do with it."

"We'll drive the truck over and cut it up and pack it in. You got a huntin' knife."

"Nah, just my filletin' knife.

"That'll work, I got my knife." He patted the sheath attached to his belt where his hunting knife was stored.

"You go get your tack and then pull up the truck."

"Sure." Wally spit.

Wally walked back toward the river bank where he had left his tackle box. He ambled slowly, muttering, "What an asshole! Christ, now we hafta gut the fuckin' thing! An' outta season, Christ almighty if the game warden comes. Why oh why do I always let myself in for this. The sonofabitch." Wally didn't want to be cutting up the elk, he wanted to be out fishing. He wanted to have a few beers, fry up a fish, take a few home.

With a grin Billy began cutting into the belly of the elk.

Wally didn't see the bear.

Billy didn't see the bear, at first. It had eaten the fish Billy had left lying on the flat stone next to the river before it clambered over the rocks and toward the edge of the meadow. To a casual observer it would have appeared to amble between the poplars and the short pines. The practiced eye would have known the Grizzly had a target. It ignored

Wally, and by stealth made its way close to where Billy worked cutting the animal.

The Grizzly came from behind. It charged at Billy. That was the moment that Billy saw the bear. His hands were deep in the guts of the elk, his thoughts on elk stew. He thought he heard a noise and said, "Wally." Then he looked over his shoulder just as the bear was a stride away. Billy screamed, all the air in his lungs bursting out, "Wally!"

In that moment the bear on was on him. Billy shrieked and lashed out with his bloodied knife. The knife got stuck in the fur, and fell from Billy's hand. Billy thought to run, but the bear had already tackled him. It was too late. Billy thought, "I'm gonna die." He tried to hit the bear on the snout. The bear didn't seem to feel it. Billy curled into a ball, his instinct telling him he had to protect his belly and his face.

It was then that Wally, who was walking towards the truck as slowly as he could, creel and tackle in hand, noticed the bear by the elk. He saw his friend being tossed about by the bear. He thought he had heard his name being called and in that instant he knew what he had heard.

Wally dropped his gear and ran to the truck, his legs catching in the grass so that he almost stumbled, but so great was his fear, so powerful the adrenaline that rushed through his body he wasn't aware of that. Wally grabbed the gun from inside the pick-up. His fingers trembled as he raised the gun up to his shoulder and put his eye to the sight. He cocked the gun and pulled on the trigger. The gun blasted, the recoil knocking Wally against the truck. His breath was pushed out of his lungs; he gasped for air. His ears rung, but he could hear Billy yelling. His brain registered the words, "shoot her again, shoot her again."

The bear surprised by the bang of the gun started up,

but only briefly. Then she felt the sting of the bullet in her hind quarter. She batted at her bottom, the blood already reddening her golden grey fur. With a look that Wally recalled in his nightmares for years after, she turned toward him. Her contempt for such a small adversary and perhaps the pain in her flank caused her to take a few steps as though undecided as to what she should do. She loped for a moment and then her gait picked up. She charged Wally.

The man, in his panic, peed and shat his pants. He ran around the open truck door and tried to jump in. The stock of the gun caught on the door. He faltered, then he threw the gun into the cab and jumped in. It was the bear that closed the door on him in one push. There she stood leaning against the cab pressing her face into the half open window, trying to claw her way into the cab. Wally pressed his back flat against the back of the other door, thinking he should kick back at the bear.

Then Wally remembered the gun. He carefully pulled the gun up from under his back and slowly turned it so that the trigger was at his fingers and the muzzle was aimed at the bear. He pulled the trigger. The gun exploded, sending the bullet down the bore; it travelled out the muzzle through the window and into the bear. The bear flew back and the gun flew up and out of Wally's hands. Wally's body was already so tightly squeezed against that door of the cab that he took the brunt of the recoil. His head hit the glass of the window, cracking it. Before flying high and landing back on top of Wally the gun cracked the bones of Wally's rib cage and bruised his chest. He lost consciousness for a moment. When he came to he had a ringing in his ears, and his head hurt like he had been on the biggest bender of his life.

All was silent, but for the chirping of birds, which Wally could not hear. Wally lifted his body. His chest ached. He noticed the wet crotch of his jeans, felt the goo in his underwear and wondered what it was. He lifted himself. His arms ached. He looked out the shattered window of the cab. The bear lay still. Across the meadow he saw the elk carcass.

Wally opened the door and slid his feet to the ground. His legs wobbled and he grabbed the door for support. It swung against him but he held firm, and when he felt sure his weight was being supported he took a step forward and then another step. Then he stopped. He had a thought. He slowly turned and reached back into the cab for the gun. Fortified with the gun he took another two steps and looked at the bear. The animal lay felled, the fur of its face and neck matted with blood, a trickle of blood slowly gurgling from its neck. Wally aimed at the bear's chest, where he hoped its heart would be. He fired the gun and heard the bang, then the thud of the bullet in the hulk of the bear. The recoil of the gun against his chest caused him to tremble with pain.

"Ouww. Shit"

The bear lay still. The forest was silent. The crow's caw caught in its craw. The squirrels hushed.

Wally walked half backward half forward trying to keep an eye on the bear. He figured bears were no stupider than humans and that maybe the bear was faking it. He'd heard of bears doing that and then tackling the fool who thought the bear was dead. But the bear didn't stir and Wally walked gingerly toward the elk. Every few steps he whispered, as though afraid to wake the bear, "Billy, Billy you alright?" But Billy didn't rouse.

His stomach began to curdle with fear, different than when the bear was after him. He began to think his friend might be dead. When he reached the elk he saw Billy pressed into the thick fur hide on the back of the elk. He was curled in a ball, like a child, his knees up to his chest and his wrists between his knees, his face hidden behind the fists of his clenched hands.

Wally went around the elk. Crouching next to Billy he steeled himself and said, "Billy." Then he touched his friend's shoulder.

Billy's body shuddered and it exploded, legs jerked out, arms splayed with such force that Wally lost his balance and was knocked over. Billy jumped up and then he ran across the meadow and into the bush. There he hid behind a tree. Once stopped he looked out at the meadow and saw Wally waving and walking towards him. Billy's legs gave way and he crumpled onto the ground hugging the tree. When Wally came up to him Wally found his friend, his teeth chattering, his eyes and cheeks wet with tears.

Wally knelt beside his friend and said, "It's ok Billy, I shot 'im, you're ok. We're gonna be ok, we're gonna be ok." Billy looked at him and then he clasped his arms around Wally, gripping his friend in a tight hug. Wally let out a holler of pain so that he let Wally go. Billy said, "What the hell?"

The pain of his chest caused tears to come to Wally's eyes. "My chest," he said and he slid to the ground. Billy sat down beside him. The two rested against each other as they sat on the ground of the forest for a time. Then Wally said, "C'mon, we better get going before another bear comes along." This spurred Billy to stand up. It was then that Wally noticed the blood trickling down Billy's back and arms.

"Jesus Billy, we gotta get you to the hospital."

He looked at the ripped cloth, the flaps of torn skin on Billy's back.

"Let's get you to the truck."

They hobbled back to the truck and Wally placed his jacket over Billy's back and seated him as comfortably as he could. Billy looked across the dashboard and out the windshield, out to the bear and beyond that to the elk.

Walking around the truck Wally thought of himself. He felt the goo in his jeans.

"Chrissake, I can't drive into town like this."

Taking the gun, he ran down to the river and dropped his jeans and Stanfields underwear. He waded into the river barely feeling the cold water. He washed himself, then he scrubbed the briefs and jeans. He put them on wet. Picking up the fishing tackle and the gun he walked back over to the truck as quickly as he could.

He started up the truck and turned on the heat.

"What took you so long?" Billy looked at his friend as he started the truck.

"Nuthin' I just picked up the tackle, made sure we didn't leave nuthin' behind."

"Smart thinkin'."

They sat without words for a goodly time as they drove back to town. Wally's teeth chattered from the cold of his wet trousers and he tried fiddling with the heating. It worked, but only lightly, so the cab warmed but did not get hot. Wally tried wiggling about a bit so that the rubbing would warm him. Billy seemed to doze; the rough road jarring him awake when the tires hit a deep pot hole. Once he said, "Shame about the elk. We shoulda tried to bring it in."

"Jesus, Billy, we gotta get you to the hospital never mind the elk."

"We'll go back tomorrow, we'll git it tomorrow." He closed his eyes and thought about how they would set out to do that.

Wally just nodded and remembered that he had to work the next day and thought Billy could go on his own if he wanted.

The young doctor at the hospital, having been on duty all of the night and that day was quick and efficient. He was tired and thought only of his bed while he cleaned the wounds and listened to Billy and Wally's tale of how they had been charged by the Grizzly and how Wally had shot the Grizzly. One of the biggest they had ever seen. There was no mention of the elk. The nurse who attended was rather more interested. She told her nurse friends and her husband and so the story spread about town of how Billy and Wally had shot a huge grizzly. Mostly people just shook their heads and said, "Ah, just a tall tale." No one mentioned it to the game warden.

The next morning Wally went to work and told all his friends about how he shot the Grizzly and how he drove Billy back to town. Billy wanted to go out in his truck and grab what was left of the elk, but his body was too sore and his stitches hurt too much, so he just looked out the window at the snow that was starting to fall. The snow fell for three days straight, so that there were a good two and a half feet in town and people said there was twice as much in the mountains. Nobody could go back into the Bull River country again that winter.

Wally didn't go fishing with Billy ever again after that. At first he didn't want to and then he didn't need to. One day during that winter, late in the season after the elk and the bear were past being stew for the bush, Wally was shopping at Overwaitea. His shopping cart was nearly full and he put a case of Tahiti Treat on top of the boxes of Captain Crunch, Kraft Dinner, Pop Tarts and Hamburger Helper. Then he went to the check out. There was a new cashier who smiled especially prettily. She started to talk to Wally and he liked the sound of her voice.

SILENCE

"Kenneth dear," Mrs. Trites Wood said, and looked over at her husband, "I know you don't care for the father, I don't like the pushy mother much either, but John seems to be a lovely young man. He is so well-mannered and when he's around Rory seems to be less sullen. I think he's a good influence."

Mrs. Trites Wood liked her son's good-looking blond friend, John Brummell. Though his manner was sometimes a touch irritating — she would have called it precious had she not liked him — he always looked at her as if she were attractive. He could even tell her she was beautiful without it sounding ingratiating and for this she was grateful. She had reached that age where she felt she could no longer take flattery from younger men for granted. Though she knew it was a silly vanity she always felt younger when he looked at her.

Her husband knit his brow, took a fierce bite of toast and mumbled, "Mmm, I'm not so sure." He had overheard suggestions that his son's friend was "a little light in his loafers" but he, too, in his reserved way liked the boy's enthusiastic nature.

Though aloof himself, Mr. Trites Wood was attracted to his wife's more passionate nature and it pleased him that his son's teenage churlishness would dissolve when John was about. Rory would become more like his mother and Mr. Trites Wood would be reminded of the happy boy who had tugged on his ears and tickled him as a child. He did not understand why his son could be so difficult at times but he remembered the loyalty of the little boy and so the father was loyal to his son even when he was unpleasant to be around. Mr. Trites Wood was often more direct when speaking to himself than he was when speaking to others. He even thought that it was probable he would like John as much as his wife did were it not for the boy's father.

Mr. Trites Wood's enmity towards Mr. Brummell was not merely dislike of the man's demeanour, it had deep roots in history. Mr. Trites Wood was one of those people who had matured in Fernie at a time when the mining, the mine managers and the miners were largely from the town. In those earlier times the mines lay close by. The coke ovens were just blocks from Mr. Trites Wood's offices. The merchants were often shareholders of the mines (he himself had once held shares); the miners and the minions of the town were more linked; and the potentates of the mine were partners in the burden of building Fernie. Now the mines were out of town and the miners were beginning to earn more than some of the merchants. The profits of the mines went to places far away — the same places that the mine managers now answered to. With the changes in the mines there had also come a new class of man who did not know the old order and this unsettled Mr. Trites Wood.

Across town, amongst the houses of the newly arrived, the new rich, and the executives of the new open pit mine, was the house of Mr. Brummell. Though not one of the mercantile princes of Fernie, Mr. Brummell was a man who had a certain control over the destiny of the town because he was a powerful executive at the mines. In some ways this made him even more mighty than Mr. Trites Wood.

Mr. Brummell came, as the townsfolk said, "From the coast". He was not a local, but the locals had to heed his word so considerable was his sway at the mine. So, though Brummell worked in Sparwood for that great prince of industry, Edgar Kaiser, he was a force to be reckoned with in Fernie. Mr. Brummell followed the dictates of the great Kaiser with a loyalty and ferocity that allowed for no thought of his own. He was the perfect vassal.

Mr. Brummell neither liked nor disliked Mr. Trites Wood, any more than he liked or disliked Fernie or for that matter the mine. What his myopic eyes envisioned through the thick black rimmed glasses he wore was a golf course under an American sun and a house in Shaughnessy in the Vancouver rain. He saw a series of moves from office to office as he climbed the ladder so that ultimately his office would come to be as close to the great Kaiser's as was possible. With a grim smile in the dark in bed at night, and despite his dedication to the Imperator of the company, he saw himself sitting in the great man's chair. Beyond this he was pleased with his wife in that she was ornamental, dedicated to helping his career and a credit when entertaining the other managers. He left her to raise their boys with the expectation that one day they would become company men like he was. Though not in his company, as he continually told his sons, "No one will think you got the job because of your old man." For Mr. Brummell was to men of his sort, a man of rectitude. He attended church regularly, sang "God Save the Queen" and "Oh Canada" and meant both as long as he sang the words. He wore his engineer's ring with pride, and generally held that the world had an order and in that order the company and the great Kaiser held priority of place for what they brought to the world.

Mrs. Brummell had only one ambition. That was, as she said to her mother, "To make my sons a credit to their father and to society." Mrs. Brummell shared her husband's opinion that a successful life included a home in Shaughnessy, and though she detested golf, she did see herself playing bridge with the ladies while the "men were out playing that silly game chasing that little white ball with sticks."

Her waking thought was for her boys and her evening prayer asked, "Dear God, please watch over my sons, John, William and Bruce and protect them from evil and harm and bless them as you have blessed me by sending them to me. Amen." The fulcrum of her day was her sons, and though the two eldest had left the house to go to university she still fussed about them. She prepared "care baskets" which were filled with home-made cookies, cakes, chocolates, Brown's beef jerky which the boys especially liked, and sometimes jars of home-made preserves. These she would tightly pack into a cardboard box using underwear and socks she had bought as stuffing so that there would be no breakage. Then she took the parcel to the post office and sent it the fastest way possible so the contents would be fresh. This took some of her time but did not in any way reduce the full glow of love she reserved for John. For him she made elaborate breakfasts so that he would be nourished and his favourite foods for dinner so that he would feel love even in her food. Her husband's dinner was left in the oven. He worked late and dined at odd hours. She knew it did not matter what he ate, for given his indifference to her cooking, he seemed to have no taste-buds left.

When not catering and provisioning for her sons Mrs.

Brummell arranged the house and cultivated the garden. All this went unnoticed by her husband who was in any event not interested in food or décor or those things which give grace to life beyond the impression they might make on his senior managers.

Her sons William and Bruce had always done as they were told to avoid their father's strict discipline but now that they were university boys they secretly despised their mother who they thought silly and obsessed with niceties. And they often spoke openly after a few drinks, of their father as "a miserable old bastard." Even though they stood to attention when the anthem was played, most of their time they spent chasing girls who were looking for the "MRS" degree and longed for the day when they would sit in the CEO chair.

John, unlike Mrs. Brummell's other boys who had been choked in the hot house tended by the mother, not only fared well, he flourished. He was an intelligent boy. He recognized his mother's devotion for what it was — the love of a mother. He looked forward to making his mother as happy as he could and thereby excited the disdain of his brothers and father alike. He also sought to please his father, when he saw him, which was irregularly and was usually a time of brooding silence.

Mr. and Mrs. Trites Wood had only one son. Rory was tall like his father, and sleek and smooth like his mother. He was named for his reddish hair which in his teens turned auburn. He had been a boisterous, cheerful, likeable boy. As he entered youth he became quiet and he often looked like he was concentrating on a difficult mathematical equation. His pleasant distinctive face might have revealed teenage insecurity had he not learned from both his parents, but particularly from his mother, the skill of controlling his expression. He always chose to appear to be serene like his mother, though his father believed, often correctly, that his expression concealed sullenness.

Hockey, painting, soccer, writing — Rory tried and tasted. His curiousity urged him to meet new people, even strangers to Fernie. But there were constants — music, skiing and John, his best friend. John had been his best friend since the first day they had met at the high school in grade 8. The boys had played together each day after school, throwing rocks into the Elk River, hiking Mt. Fernie, riding along the highway, sitting on the T-bar up to tower 24 and getting off and skiing down the Bear run, the one challenging the other to go faster or take a bigger jump. Each day the boys spent in the harmony of youth that allows no discordance to disturb the melody of their affection. As boyhood ended and the two grew through pubescence their affection increased and took on the mature resonance of two young men who were devoted to one another. The boys went on double dates with the prettiest girls of the town. They went to drive-in movies and they went to the Hiway Café where they began to plan their university careers.

Like some boys in early puberty they had the habit of relieving sexual tension in one another's presence. The first time it happened was in the summer at the Trites Wood summer cabin at Rosen Lake. Rory's mother had driven to town for groceries and the two boys were left alone.

It was a hot July day, its stillness exaggerated by their tug-o-war on the wharf as the two teens pushed and pulled one another into the water. The weight of the sky flattened their splashes. The cold of the water was not cooling and in the course of wrestling they developed erections. John had been having erections for a few months already and knew from his older brother, Bruce, how to tease what pleasure could be extracted by hands appropriately applied. He said to Rory, "C'mon inside, I'll show you how to wrestle down Danger the one eyed Ranger."

"What? Wrestle who?"

"You know, c'mon." And John walked towards the cabin.

Rory was embarrassed. He had an inkling of what John meant because of talk he had heard, but he still wasn't quite sure of what was going on. The only thing he knew was that he could trust John. Nervously he said, "Sure."

They went into the dark cool cabin, through the sitting room and into the bunk room they shared. There John removed his red Speedo and stood with his erection touching his stomach. "You too." He whispered to Rory.

"Are you sure we should. What if someone comes?" Though he had seen John naked many times it was the first time that he consciously took note of the other's body.

"Don't talk crazy, no one's gonna come."

"Okay." Rory slipped out of his tight blue bathing suit. John looked at Rory and wolf whistled. "Let's jack off."

"What do you mean?"

"You know, pull the pud."

John began to stroke himself. Rory looked at John with momentary disbelief, then with uncertainty. John did not stop. His silly grin and the continuing erection Rory felt led him to imitate his friend, at first timidly and then with equal gusto.

It was the first time, but not the last. Every now and then, particularly after horseplay, they would repeat the adventure they had first experienced at the lake. As they became more mature teens they resisted this mutual experience becoming more embarrassed as they grew older not daring to look at one another during or after the act.

In time they stopped completely, unless they had been drinking. Then one or the other of them would recall their boyish efforts. In their drunken state they would re-enact their search for relief. Invariably this followed a routine. They would go on a double date. Sitting in Rory's car they would neck and pet with the girls they had taken out on the date. After dropping the girls at their homes they would drive up the Burmis road, or to the end of the Cokato road. They parked in the dark, guzzled a bottle of whiskey or vodka and talked about how sexy their girls were. The talk would become more slurred and more crude, until it was time to relieve their "blue balls". They would laugh with drunken bravado and before too much longer, with eyes looking straight ahead out of the car window, they would finish the job their exertions with the girls had begun.

One autumn afternoon Rory punched John's arm in the way that one jock playfully punches another. Knowing the exact feel of the punch, John turned without surprise and grinned, his eyes radiating such complete trust that they left Rory slightly breathless.

"Got time for coffee later?"

"Hmmm, not really, but for you."

"Why, what's up?"

"Not much, I just want to go for coffee with you." Rory leaned in so that his arm brushed John's. It was all the touching they allowed themselves when they were anywhere others could see them. It was not something they had discussed, it had just happened.

"The girls'll wanna come too. I told Christine I'd meet her after school to study trig."

"I suppose… they can come too."

It was in the late days of October, when the rains of autumn brooded low so that the clouds of mist played at the edges of the forest teasing the boughs with hints of sleet. Rory and John had, after coffee at the Hi-Way Café, dropped their girlfriends at home.

"I don't want to go home yet, let's go cruising," suggested John quietly.

Rory didn't say anything. He turned the car in the direction of Main Street. As they drove down the empty street, John fiddled with the radio. CFEK blared "Good Bye Yellow Brick Road".

"I don't want to cruise Main, Rory."

"Okay, where to then Mr. Weisenheimer?"

"How about let's go to the river."

"Sure."

They parked under the dark boughs of a pine tree, the drops of rain plopping dried needles onto the windscreen, the evening sky darkening.

The music from the radio was interrupted by the yattering of the dj. Rory turned it off. The two looked at one another. It happened quickly. John leaned in to Rory and placed his lips on those of his friend. Neither one moved. Their lips touched, then pressed hard. They pulled away from one another but did not let go, and then their lips touched again.

It was in that moment that John understood that his world had changed. That he was no longer who he had been the moment before the kiss. This was a change deeper than the change that a boy has when he becomes a man — he knew who he was. It was only later that he realized that every plan he had had for his life would now be different. At the time he began to tremble with fear, and he shook as he leaned in to kiss Rory again.

On the lips of his lover John felt a protection and comfort that he had not known since he curled up in his mother's lap when he was an infant. He felt that so long as Rory was there he could be strong and stable and certain, but the minute that Rory left he began to feel dizzy, as though he could feel the spin of the earth as it teeter tottered on its axis. He would need to hold onto something. His breath would stop and then he could inhale in ragged gulps. Even sports did not give him relief. He would run after a ball, skate for a puck, but no matter how hard he exerted himself the balls or the pucks kept moving. When he ran to them he found nothing there.

At night he lay in bed and prayed. He did not pray to be changed. He prayed that he might be beside Rory all the next day, that Rory would not leave him alone. He could not bear to be out of Rory's sight, such was the uncertainty of the cosmos, and the certainty of what he saw in Rory. He wanted to feel that he should blame Rory for this, because Rory had let him kiss him. Rory had not shunned him, but then John remembered his own longing for that kiss. He could not and did not want to fool himself.

Nights became a feverish delirium of waiting to see Rory. Showering, dressing, eating breakfast became the automatic movements of a body moving through time. What did he know of them? He chose the clothes he put on according to Rory's compliments. If Rory said John looked good in a particular shirt or trousers then John liked to wear that shirt or trousers, even though he thought how silly he was, behaving like a girl.

Rory was affected by their changed relationship in the way an aristocrat might have felt — confident his love was good, certain that he was noble, therefore that to love in this way was noble too. Rory understood his love was pure and true and would remain so as long as he did nothing to sully it by touching another woman or man in the way he touched John.

So they continued for a time, kissing but nothing more.

Their love had made them chaste. They seemed to know that the time was not right for there to be more. They made music together, Rory strumming his guitar and humming, John making up lyrics to the music and singing the words. They were simple songs about the mountains, and skiing in fresh snow. They were love songs though neither used the word love so as not to embarrass the other. Sometimes they would lie on the bed in John's room, their arms locked in a tight hug, their lips joined, listening to music on the record player, or to the sound of the wind, or to the silence of the house.

Rory did not see Mr. Brummell, as he rushed to the bed and grabbed Rory by the hair, pulling his head up from John's. Then he struck Rory so hard that he fell from the bed. In the first instant Rory was surprised and stunned. He raised himself from the floor. He saw Mr. Brummell looking at him with eyes wide, red with anger, his lips a tight black line. Rory saw a hatred that was so intense that he knew evil for the first time. Rory did not cower, he drew himself up.

"Get out! Get out of my house!! I never want to see you here again.

"No dad!"

"Shut up you cur." Mr. Brummell breathed deeply, "You will never see each other again."

"No dad, please, I can't live without Rory."

"I'm not having you turn my son into a Nancy boy."

"Mr. Brummell, don't do this."

John saw contempt in his father's eyes, something he had never seen before.

"We love each other." Rory placed the fact before the three of them. John and Rory exchanged a glance. For a moment it was as though Mr. Brummell had been slapped.

His face turned a deep purple with white splotches and he turned as though looking for escape.

"Shut up, you disgust me." He grabbed Rory's arm, and shoved him towards the door. "Get out."

"Don't go." John began to fight back tears, trying to be manly in front of his father. His effort constricted each sob, tearing at his stomach. He wanted to wretch, a gag of bile rising in his throat. His fear that Rory would leave compelled him to try to breathe, the air trapped by the tightening of his chest. His face began to turn red and then white as he choked on his humiliation, rage, helplessness.

He got up from the bed and walked towards Rory. His father pushed him back onto the bed.

"You stay there."

Rory lunged at Mr. Brummell.

Seeing the boy make a fist Mr. Brummell grabbed Rory's arm. "Get out, get out before I kill you."

Rory looked at John.

"Go." John's blue eyes shimmered. He looked at his father with defiance as though the tears had rid him of fear.

Rory shook his head, "No, No." His shirt tore as he tried to pull away from John's father who then struck him on the chest. Rory tried to hit back. Enraged Mr. Brummell began to shake him. Fearing that his father might kill Rory, John yelled, "Go, Rory, go!"

Rory yanked free of John's father but stopped at the door and said, "You sure."

John nodded.

Rory moved slowly and deliberately, his head straight, his back rigid, his pace even as he walked along the corridor, down the stairs, across the foyer and out the door of the house. In the driveway he saw Mrs. Brummell who was getting out of her car.

"Good evening Mrs. Brummell."

"Why hello Rory, nice evening?"

He smiled, rather oddly she thought. "I hope so," he said. Then he got into his car and drove home.

John sat on his bed, his head hung. He did not dare to look at his father's face; he did not want to see the look of contempt.

"Son, I know you're no namby pamby. What did that boy do to make you do it?"

John remained silent.

"Well it makes no difference; you'll never see him again."

John did not shift his gaze from the patch of cloth that had been torn from Rory's shirt and lay, a little blue tatter, on the beige carpet.

"You're going to boarding school. Enough of this nonsense. They'll teach you to be a man there."

"No, Dad, I want to stay here."

"This is not a discussion. I'm telling you what's going to happen. If you don't do as I tell you I'll go to the police and tell them exactly what happened. I will have them charge that disgusting fairy. "

"You'd never…. If they charge him, they have to charge me. I'll tell them exactly how I love him. "

The father grabbed his son's head between his hands, and held his face so close that John could see the flecks of red in the blue of his father's eyes. "Oh son, son." Then tears began to stream down the father's face.

"I'm sorry, I can't help it." The boy's voice cracked. "I…" he paused, "love Rory."

The father looked uncomprehendingly at his son. "Men cannot love men," he said.

"But I do."

"No, no, no! No son of mine does."

John grasped his father by the wrists and pulled the man's heavy hands from his face.

"You're just confused. All boys have good friends they love. But that's it, it's just puppy love. You wait and see. One day you'll meet a girl and then you'll fall in love for real."

John smiled. The comforting tone in his father's voice sounded absurd, as though his father was speaking in a foreign tongue. Then he said, "Yeah, sure Dad, maybe."

Relieved to hear acquiescence, his father smiled back and said, "See there, that's better, now you're talking sense. Let's not mention this to your mother. We don't want to upset her."

The next morning Rory waited in the school parking lot in his car. He sat and watched as teachers and students arrived and he waited for John to come. Sometimes John walked. At other times his mother dropped him off, but he always came over to the car where Rory waited for him. The bell rang and still John didn't come. Rory began to feel a tightness in his stomach. He wondered if he should drive over to John's house. But he wasn't sure if that would help.

Rory had not slept the night before. Not that he was so much afraid of Mr. Brummell, he simply could not imagine what the man might really do. He could not see what could be done. Two boys had kissed, what could anyone do? But in the darker moments of that night Rory knew that John's father could cause trouble. The man was crass. Would he go to his parents and expose Rory and John's love? Would he go to the police? That might be trouble, but what would the police do with two boys who had kissed. Rory could not fathom what anyone might do. How could two pairs of lips joining lead to trouble?

John did not think as Rory did. Each molecule of his body felt acutely alert. John did not think. He felt. He saw images. Over and over he saw the image of Rory as though a seraphim. Rory was calling him, calling him to come. But where to? He saw the face of his mother, love radiating from her eyes. Then he saw her face as it would look if she were to think of him kissing Rory. He saw the face of his father the day they golfed together. He remembered how proud his father looked when he hit a long drive. Then his synapses fired and flared as he remembered the look on his father's face in that moment when his father realized he had seen John kiss Rory.

In his father's eyes was a look that John had never seen before. He saw old decrepit eyes with a cataract on the retinas like a hole in dirt where maggots and centipedes and roots and worms macerate failure — the failure of having raised a son who could kiss a man. As though his own measure as a man was defined by this one thing. But John could also read despair in those eyes, the despair of a father who recognized that he hated his son for this one thing: a kiss. John saw all this and in that instant when he looked up over Rory's shoulders he heard in his father's glance a howl of such anguish that it hurt John's ears though there had been no sound at all.

Rory's call disappeared in the din in John's head. He sensed that if Rory would come he might bear it, but Rory did not come.

That night John placed a chair next to the trunk of the great Mountain Ash in his parent's garden. With a graceful sweep he flung a rope over the bough of the tree. The rope landed sure. John gripped it and pulled. His hands did not tremble. His body knew the steps. Each atom united in the flight from madness. He no longer thought of anything beyond wanting silence. This was not a conscious thought, it was a physical response. The molecules of each cell of his being wanted to stop their vibration. They wanted rest. They wanted to be still. His spirit and his mind wanted complete, uninterrupted silence. In that mortal din he wanted peace. He tied the knot. He slipped the noose over his head. He kicked the chair away. His grunt. Violated silence.

Mrs. Trites Wood heard the news from Mrs. Arthur Young. Violet Young had been at the meat market. It was after she and Mrs. Greenleaf, the Reverend's wife, had left the premises and were standing in the street where they could not be overheard that Mrs. Greenleaf told her. Mrs. Young had not even bothered to disguise her emotion on hearing the news. She bade her friend goodbye and walked as quickly as she could to the Trites Wood house. Instinctively she knew that this news would be best brought by her to her friend Mrs. Trites Wood. As she rang the door bell, she wondered how to phrase the words she knew had to be said. The door was answered by Mrs. Trites Wood herself. Even as she sought to remain composed Violet noted how perfect Mrs. Trites Wood's coiffure was. She observed that she was dressed in an Escada suit, despite the early hour of the day.

"Violet, what a surprise!"

"Sorry to bother you at such an early hour."

"Nonsense, my dear, come in. I was just going to do my letters, but how much nicer it will be to sit with you."

"Thank you."

They walked into the sitting room which Violet thought the most tasteful sitting room, next to her own, in town.

"Please sit." Mrs. Trites Wood stood before the little settee in front of the fireplace.

"I'll just bring us some coffee, or would you prefer a tea?"

"Thanks, no nothing. I can't stay long, but I must speak with you."

"Are you sure you wouldn't like even a glass of water?"

"No, no my dear."

Mrs. Trites Wood detected a faint hysteria that she had never before heard in her friend's voice.

She seated herself next to Violet who had not removed her coat, though she adjusted her scarf.

"Now what is it?"

"Sarah, I don't quite know how to say it, but I have just heard the most terrible news and I thought you should hear it from me before all others."

Mrs. Trites Wood raised her eyebrow thinking how often she had heard it rumoured that her husband was having an affair and wondering if this was the news that would follow. Her brow was untroubled for if there was one thing she knew with certainty it was that her husband was as dedicated to her as he had always been, much as some women might seek to catch his eye.

Violet's voice was but a whisper. "Sarah, I've just heard that John Brummell took his life." Her eyes teared, for though she did not know the boy well, and cared not one jot for his parents, she had seen him with Rory. And she knew enough to know that misfortune was about to enter the house of her friend.

Sarah Trites Wood sat motionless for a moment. Then she leaned toward her friend and said, "How can that be?"

"I don't know, but I just heard it from Ivy and she no doubt had it from the Reverend."

"Oh."

Violet looked at the woman who, despite her wet eyes, sat perfectly straight. This unnerved Violet and she felt she had to say something more, say something that might help.

"Sarah, I told Ivy, and I was as firm as I could be, that she mustn't say a word to anyone about the boy taking his own life. Who needs to know that? It's bad enough as it is."

"Thank you Violet." Mrs. Trites Wood pressed the hand that was laid on her arm.

Mrs. Trites Wood would not later be able to recall how the rest of the morning passed. Though she went through the motions of early day in her residence she thought of only one thing and that was how she would tell her son.

It was noon before she saw Rory. As he nearly always did on school days, he came home for lunch. Often he came with John. Often the three of them would sit together at the kitchen table and they would share soup, sandwiches, salad or the like. She had taken to laying three places every day. When the three of them sat at the table she laughed with Rory and John as they told her stories of boyhood adventures or they would listen with unfeigned attention as she told them of her own immigrant childhood.

She stood at the kitchen window looking by turn at the room with its white cupboards and gingham curtains, at the table and then out the mullioned glass panes. A plate of ham and cheese sandwiches, Rory's favourite, was placed on the pretty checked table cloth. There were two places set. Her back was very straight, her head held tall. She looked out at as her son parked his car in the drive and sauntered toward the kitchen door.

His grin as he walked in the door, unsettled her. During some moments of the morning she had thought, even hoped, that he might already know.

"Hi Mama." He kissed her cheek, and swung into the seat on her right, grabbed a sandwich from the plate and took a bite. He looked at her and said with a slight tremor of nervousness, "John didn't come to school this morning."

His mother looked at him with tears in her eyes.

"I know."

He gazed at her more intently, his eyes more alert.

"You know? What do you know?" He thought of the afternoon before, of the ecstasy and then the face of John's father. He hadn't heard from John since.

She came over to the table and pulled her chair next to his, so close that the curve of the wooden seats of each chair touched. She took his hand and, holding it tightly, said, "Rory my love. John," and her voice cracked so that each word sounded like kindling being snapped, "John is dead."

He looked at her. He pulled his hand from hers, and jumped from his chair knocking it over so that it hit the chequered tiles of the floor with a slap. He began to run across the room. His hip hit the china cabinet, dishes rattling. He bounced from the cabinet and ran into the washstand, then against the door. He stomped around the room in circles that grew ever smaller. Finally he stopped. He fell before his mother, grabbing her legs and wrapping his arms around them tightly, his head resting in her lap. His body convulsed and she heard him say the word, "No" and again "no" and again "no". An incantation, a plea. He did not stop, and she let him continue even when he began to sob. They sat for an hour or longer. She stroked his hair and he held onto her until finally the "no's" became silent, and yet she could hear them. Finally he looked up at her face and said, "I love him." She looked at him, her eyes clear. He could see how his pain hurt her, and she said, "I know. I know."

Some people say that no one ever knows for certain why anyone would commit suicide. Perhaps it is better so. There are those who know with certainty the cause. For them the pain must be greater. It was so for Mr. Brummell and Rory. Mr. Brummell never told anyone what he had seen or where he was certain what he had seen had led. The Brummell's soon left Fernie and were never heard of again.

The Trites Woods stood together at the funeral held at St. Margaret's Cemetery. Rory did not look at either Mr. or Mrs. Brummell. He looked for a moment at the hole into which the casket would be lowered. He looked at the casket. He held his parents' hands and this supported him. That night he left his house when it was dark and walked to the grave. He lay on top of it, his wails breaking the silence of the night. Then he too was still. By the light of morning he left the grave and went home.

Mrs. Trites Wood said to her husband, "We must send Rory to Europe this summer." Her husband nodded.

CHRISTMAS IN FERNIE

"When I was a boy there were two colours that were Fernie: one was black and the other white."

The children sitting around the table, belt buckles straining from too much turkey and stuffing and sweet potato pie and four cookies and a bowl of Granny's Yule log Ice-cream look at me and wonder what their old uncle is talking about. But I know.

"Everyone from those times knows what they were, those two colours. The black was coal and the white was snow and no two other colours speak of that time like black and white. The black was what everyone lived on. From the great houses of the merchant class and the mine masters to the smallest miners' shacks, everyone needed the black coal that came from the ground and cost backs and lungs and lives but put bread and butter on the table. Everyone feared the ringing of the bell that signaled another death, but the brave who loved mining and those without the imagination to find a way out, still went down into the pits.

"They came back up every day if they were lucky. Their clothes and faces were black and they were ugly and they frightened me. But once the men were cleaned, and on their way to the bar, their wives in curlers yelling from the door that they not be late, they took on an exotic Arabian cast. At the lash their eyes were trimmed with heavy black lines and they looked like kohl-smeared faux-Arab lovers, mal-faced Valentinos, except for the young handsome miners who carried this miners' mark with bravado.

"The miners were never blacker than when they came out of the pits and it had snowed. The crows counted each one like a black brother, in caws which made me think of the cackles of Madam Lafarge, as their claws stamped the snow from the boughs of the trees. Or perhaps they were just complaining about that white that fell from above, out of clouds that pushed over the mountain peaks. Clouds that were cocooned on all sides by stone and pines and seemed content to settle and rest their burden of flakes until the snow erased every mark of the labour of man in the mines.

"The snow in Fernie then was whiter, deeper, and lay longer than it does now. It would stick in nooks and crannies and crevices and curl around eaves. It would pile so high between houses that neighbours who during other seasons looked out windows to greet one another could only see grey blue walls of ice. At least that's what the old men said.

"It would snow, sometimes as early as Halloween or even before, and I can remember ghosts in white sheets running through the streets becoming apparitions in the billowing gusts of snowflakes that whipped around the white pillow cases they held in mittened hands. And I remember how the snow and wind would steal the "trick or treat" yelled at the top of our voices so those who gave candies couldn't hear our appeal.

"When the first snow fell we ran after snowflakes and caught them on our tongue. I remember the taste of the cold ice petals melting on my hot tongue. It was a treat as good as ice cream. We ran until our tongues were sore from stretching the tips up to reach flake after flake.

"I remember our footsteps after a fresh snow fall. We would stamp our feet as we trod so that the eiderdown snow flew and left an impression of a giant foot print. Grizzly feet we would grin. Sometimes we would walk from the street up to a wall of a house and then retrace our steps so that it looked as though a spectre had entered the house through the wall.

"The snow fell and it fell and it fell, so that by Christmas there was so much snow that the old men on their stools in the pubs began to talk of their never having seen so much snow.

"In those days the walkways to the houses were precisely cut passages through a white tiramisu sprinkled with black coal dust and soot. The walkways were ice, even after we scraped and scraped. There were no snow blowers and blades on trucks. It was we children who shoveled those passages that sometimes grew so high as to be tunnels out of which we came like Inuit. Our Igloos were made of wood but the doors were ice. Shoveling those walks were chores. The lucky amongst us got a nickel or a dime a week for an allowance for doing the chores like chopping the wood and making the fire. The unlucky got nothing.

"But rich or poor, young or old, everyone in Fernie, even the curmudgeons, knew when Christmas was coming. And even those who hated the snow could not keep up their aversion at Christmas, except for one teacher I remember who was silly and wore her hair too high. Her lipstick was bright red. One day her pretty pouty lips became a frown that did not stop. She complained that the only place she wanted to be was Florida, that Fernie was "hell on earth". I guess she is there now. Her skin a slack brown. Her lips sagging along the ground from a life-time of complaints and cigarettes.

"For the rest of us, especially the children, the coming of the Christmas season was the beginning of a miracle. For me it was a miracle bigger than the Christ child, though I will own that might have been a more interesting miracle if there hadn't been a Christmas pageant to perform in each year. That evening I stood as a scratching sheep or as a shepherd in sheets or, worst of all, as an angel with aluminum foil wings. A halo of prickly tinsel garland wrapped around wire that cut into the skin of my head so that I began to understand the suffering of Jesus and his thorns. Or that evening when lines as simple as *'C' is for the Christ Child borne in a manger low* became a tongue twister that made saying *Sally sells seashells by the seashore* three times fast seem like an easy thing to do. Or that evening when Mrs. Donnershof-Smith leaned in too closely to hug me for being the 'best Joseph ever' smothering me in her ample bosom, her *Parfum de Paris* leaving me gasping for air and my head swirling.

"The pageant was the thorn on the rose of the miracle of Santa Claus. And what a miracle it was. In those days there were but three times a year you might see Santa if you were lucky. The most important, of course, was on Christmas Eve if you woke in the middle of the night and happened to catch a glimpse of his sleigh and reindeer after he had left your presents. You definitely didn't want to be awake before he came because he might not stop at your house. But once he had come you gambled that it wasn't likely that he'd come back and take the presents away. Although I never saw him on Christmas Eve and I know of no one who did. Boastful

Eddie always used to say he was sure he saw him. But no one relied on Eddie who was known to say that he 'knew a kid from Greece' and things like that which we all knew couldn't be true because Eddie had never been away from Fernie and none of us knew a kid from Greece.

"Of the other times of winter when there was a chance to see Santa, one was at the church pageant or at school. Neither of these was as reliable as the Santa who appeared on Christmas Eve. Certainly the results of the encounter were less satisfactory. The Santa who came to visit the school and the church came less well-stocked and a visit with him was brief. A few words exchanged for a mere bag of sugar candies or cookies or, on a good year, an orange.

"But there was a visit to Fernie by Santa that was always satisfactory. Every girl and boy who could possibly get there, even boys and girls from Hosmer, Coal Creek, Cokato, and Morrissey and the odd lucky child from Michel whose parents had taken them on the train to visit Fernie would queue to see the Santa who came to the Trites Wood Company Ltd. store. The dark magnificent edifice that guarded over the shopping street of Fernie was for many in those days the largest store they would ever see — in their lives.

"By the time of my childhood the store was a shabbier version of its original glorious construction. The big lettering on the crown moulding heralding its name had faded from white to grey and the crown moulding had bled from dignified brown to rust. The awnings that were unrolled on sunny days were a little frayed. Inside the wooden floors were black from scrubbing and the stately white pillars were stained and scratched. Yet it was our own little Harrods. It had men's, women's and children's clothing, dry goods, tools, and merchandise and a candy counter and food hall.

We thought that no grander purveyor of goods could exist anywhere but here in Fernie. And for us no day in that emporium was more magnificent than the day on which Santa came to visit the children at the Trites Wood & Co. store.

"The arrival of the Trites Wood Santa was as certain as Christmas Eve. We children climbed the grand stairs passing the offices where the proprietor would stand in his black suit, his watch chain glistening gold across his girth, his legs planted firmly as he composed a smile amongst the worried lines of his face. It must have been difficult to run that store in a town with so many wishes and so little money. But smile at each child he did, despite an excess of plum pudding at lunch and a tie grown too tight. Once past the forbidding office there was another flight of stairs to climb and at the top of those stairs, there, in a toy wonderland amongst colourful wrapped boxes and tinsel on a big white and red throne, sat Santa. His big belly was swathed in red and girdled in by a belt of black with a big silver buckle. On his head he wore a big red cap with a white pompom on the end. His face was round, his eyes were round and in the bush of his white beard his lips made a little round circle of red. They were just barely visible when he listened to an appeal for an especially big gift from someone very small sitting on his broad lap.

"We stood in line to see him. Jostling one another as our parents gossiped beside us, pulling ears and wiping noses, so that for an instant we could sit on his lap and tell him what we wanted for Christmas. He would laugh in a round throaty way so that his belly threatened to push the bigger children off his lap and ask 'Have you been a good boy?'

"I would sometimes think Santa looked a lot like Mr. Harold who was a widower and who lived alone and smelled of clothes worn too long. He was an old man who always had a kind smile or candy for children. Yet I would forget about this similarity when one of Santa's elves gave us a bag with the best sort of candies — Jumbo Mint Sticks, Root Beer Barrels, Taffy, Red Hots that were really red and hot, Sugar Daddys, Black Licorice Whips and jaw breakers that really broke your jaw. And chocolates in silver and gold foil and candy canes like red and white ribbons wrapped around a miniature walking stick. And always an orange sweeter than any other orange I have ever eaten.

"I remember whispering into Santa's ear that I wanted a train set, and sure enough that Christmas there was a train set under the tree for me. He was the best Santa I ever saw, but I must have been an exceptionally good boy that year."

My tiny niece, the one who looks like Cindy Lou Who, peeps up from her melting bowl of Yule Log and daringly asks "Why didn't you ask for skis?"

"Skis," I laugh with a snort. "Don't be shocked, but we did not ski. Oh there were a few fool hardy people usually from the big houses who would take long wooden skis and go to the slopes and climb up them and then ski down and they would talk about how they had skied at Sunshine or Banff. No one I knew skied, but we tobogganed. We tobagooned like I see no one brave enough to do today."

"We crazy carpet," boasts a tallow-haired nephew at the back of the table, "I pushed my carpet real fast yesterday."

I blow back, "We tobogganed on the Ridgemont Hill or on the slopes next to the river. But those magnificent tracks are all gone now under houses and roads where BMW's and Mercedes swoop in our place. We ran up the slopes like deer jumping and springing and then we careened down even faster until we were wet inside from sweat and steaming outside from the melting ice and snow on our woolens.

"I remember there never was a bigger toboggan jump than the one built by Big Boy Stevie, who was not so bright but was ever so strong. Big Boy, who was as kind as he was big, always protected us from the bullies in front of the Northern Hotel and he always asked us to go tobogganing with him. He loved speed and so he would go to the longest steepest slope that he could find. He climbed to the highest spot from where he would holler at the top of his voice, 'See you at the bottom!!' He would run and then jump onto his toboggan so that it had real tempo before he even started down the slide and he would always be at the bottom faster than any of us.

"Then one year, the day after Christmas, the year I got a new toboggan made of steel, he decided to build a jump. He carried milk pails of snow about half way up the slope and he packed the snow so that the jump was hard. The jump was higher than I am now. Its lip taunted us to dare, but we stamped and laughed and said 'you go first'. Then Big Boy asked me for my toboggan. I gave it to him and he took the jump, cautiously at first, with not too much speed. On his second try he took it with more speed.

"He took it with so much speed that the toboggan flew through the air way above our heads. Big Boy must have panicked or the momentum was too much for him because he and the toboggan separated. The toboggan shot on ahead of him like a stone from a sling shot and when it hit the ground it kept sliding right to the bottom of the hill where it kept on going, crossing into the streets of the town, puzzling motorists startled by the unsaddled steed of the snow.

"Big Boy flew up high with screams of what might have been delight or terror, doing somersaults in the air like a burly angel falling from heaven with wings clipped mid flight. He landed on his back about twenty feet down the hill. He did not stir and at first we laughed but when he still didn't get up we ran down to where he lay. His eyes were open to the sky. At first they seemed oblivious to the falling snowflakes melting into the blue, then he blinked with a sputter. Saying nothing he sat up, inhaled and inhaled again. Then he stood up and walked down the hill to his home and after that day he was never seen on the slopes again. Some say he saw God on that final flight of his. Others say his brain got knocked loose. Not long after he went to work in the mine and they say he was never happier than when he sat eating his lunch in the silence of a dark tunnel"

"What did you eat for Christmas?" asked my biggest nephew who had a second and then a third helping of the Yule log.

"What did we eat for Christmas! We had a feast every year. Your Grandma, she was in the kitchen from morning to night. Some years, when times were good, there would be a turkey with stuffing and cranberries and apple pies and in the other years there would be a joint of venison as we might call it today. But then it was just the deer that had been shot before the snow fell, with the best piece left for Christmas, and the dressing was wild saskatoons and huckleberries that we had picked in the summer.

"There was always Grandpa's smoked trout which he caught in the Elk River and smoked himself. But my favourites were the plums, peaches and pears from Creston canned in glass jars. I thought they were the sun caught and preserved and stored in perfect rows that gave the dark cellar a burst of colour and which reminded us, as we ate them, of the summer that had been and which gave promise of the one to come.

"No matter how bad the time, there were always ginger bread men and butter tarts and plum pudding. Every year I helped your Grandma take a plate of baking and Christmas dinner to old Mrs. Tolley who had too many cats. She wore bright red rouge on her creased cheeks and painted black gashes of eyebrows so that she looked like a shriveling mime, except that she had a voice that sounded like wet clothes scrubbed on a washboard. She always gave me a sweet for which I politely thanked her and which I put in my pocket and then later left on a fence post for the crows.

"After our visit to Mrs. Tolley we came straight home. Grandpa would be waiting for us and our Auntie Agnes, who wasn't an Aunt but who we called Auntie Agnes for as long as I could remember. With her came her lodger, Georgie, though folks whispered he didn't use his own bed. Mr. Samgrass came, too, with his head as round and bald as a snowman and a mouth that was dour but which told stories I did not understand until I was much older. There would also be any odd stray new friend Grandma or Grandpa took a fancy too. There were many young men who came to work in the mines for a bit and often they boarded in our spare room.

"Finally Christmas dinner was served but only after grace which Grandpa would say with dignity yet brevity so that it sounded like a sigh of relief when we said 'Amen' in unison. Then we would eat and eat and eat until the men had to loosen their belt buckles and the women would pull at mysterious places under their dresses which I thought they called "griddles" and which made me think of pancakes.

"We would sit around the table and the adults would talk of Christmases past and tell stories of the old country or of people who had died long ago, until, after her sherry with dinner and her brandy after dinner, Auntie Agnes would totter to the piano and play Christmas carols. We would sing the old tunes: *Three Ships came Sailing, Good King*

Wenceslaus, Hark the Herald Angels Sing, Away in a Manger and we always finished with *Silent Night*.

"One would have thought the evening might have ended on a peaceful note with goodwill towards all men, but once Auntie Agnes had wiped the tear that Gruber's melody left on her cheek, she would play *Oh Danny Boy*. We would all sing along as more tears traced her cheeks as she thought of old Eire and blew her nose into a flowered handkerchief.

"Then, as though that memory brought back her youth when her hair was not bottle black and she was a beauty and the boys would ride from far to court her, she would fire out an old jig. The men would begin to stamp their feet and Grandma and Grandpa would dance about the room knocking the chairs and the tree so that the glass ornaments would jingle.

"When the joy was done, Georgie would whistle through his missing teeth. 'Agnesth can you play *Sthe Christmas Balls are a hanging in sthe Pickle Barrel*.' Auntie Agnes would laugh and shout back, 'If you can siffle it I can play it.' They all laughed and I laughed too, but had no idea why. And then suddenly the hour was late and it was time for bed, and I would try to stretch the evening by saying long goodnights to all the company, but Grandma was firm, 'To bed young man.'

"To bed it was. I would climb up the stairs to my room from where I heard the laughter grow quieter and the guests began to leave and then there was the hum of *Silent Night* as Grandma came to tuck me in, promising me another day tomorrow. And silent the night was, no train whistles and shunting of coal cars, just the dark night, crows roosting in the mountain ash and the snow glistening white under the moon."

THE BAKER'S WIFE

In the Fernie of my youth there was a baker. The baker made honey glazed donuts so good that my brother, on the way to school each morning, would buy a dozen and eat six on the walk and the other six at school. I have not tasted such perfect donuts for decades now. The baker had a wife; not a robust round woman who stood behind the counter and sold donuts, with flour in her hair and a juicy piece of gossip for each of the ladies who came for their morning bread. The wife was dark-haired and womanly, with eyes that were big and round and deep brown, even darker than her hair; eyes that always had a ready laugh barely concealed behind their lustre. She must have been a very pretty girl and by the time I came to know her she was a woman in the full ripeness of life. She was a teacher, and I hope you will think neither more nor less of her because of this. I do not know if the baker and his wife loved one another; but I do know that they were together everyday of their lives until the day the baker stopped breathing. I could not be at his funeral, not because I did not want to be, but because the baker died when I was far away.

I have many-a-time had to travel away from my revered mountains and over the years I have not often seen the baker's wife. At the most perhaps once or twice a year. When I do she always has a kind word for me, and always her eyes, though they never laugh like they once used to, shine to welcome me back. Every now and then I enquired for news of her and I heard that she continued her work, teaching the children of the village as though they were her own grandchildren. I heard too that she had found solace in painting. I tracked down some of her work, and it was good, and I purchased some pieces that hang on the walls of my brother's house. I watched as she in her quiet but firm way sought to help save the village from tawdry development. I looked on as she carried placards at protests to save our hospital. I heard how she, in a patient teacherly voice, begged politicians at hearings to spare us from Coal Bed Methane. I realized one day she held us, like she held her son from his birth, in her bosom and would not suffer us to be hurt.

There will be those amongst you, certainly the young, who will say with voices strident, why do you refer to such an independent and vibrant woman as "the baker's wife"? And I will tell you, whether it is good or bad, that in old Fernie the woman was the wife of the man who she married. But I will also tell you that there is a much deeper reason. For this woman was no ordinary woman, and she, like the baker, was made to nourish. The flour on her apron was of a different kind than was that of her husband, but it was no less nourishing to our little village. And this is the story of how I know that.

The baker and his wife had a son. He was a rolly polly

little boy, as the sons of bakers often were in those days. "It was," the baker chortled, "a hazard of the trade." The boy's eyes were dark and laughed like his mother's, his hair was thick and had her colour too, but with curls that were tight and almost hinted at some trace of Africa in them. He was a good little boy and I recall playing with him when there was time in between my ever present chores or homework. I remember lying one night on the grass in the garden of the court house with him. The Courthouse of Fernie is to a boy's eye a perfect castle, a majestic back drop for unfolding dreams of knights in shining armour, dreams of King Arthur and of Lancelot and Guinevere. As the sun set, we caroused and jousted before that chateau of justice. It was an autumn evening and the mountain ashes, that to this day surround the building, had fruit as big as cherries; ripe and red so that even in the dark we could see them. We lay in the grass looking at the stars and we dreamed the dreams that boys of eleven will dream. There just at the edge of the last days of childhood, measured by how much our mothers and fathers were still our heroes, we began to aspire to be men.

I would not leave you with the impression that I grew to know the baker's son well over the years we were together, but he was always present. I likely saw him each day at school, for we were in the same grade, and we travelled down the same corridors though often entered different doors. And when there was time we would talk, not like complete strangers; rather like passengers on a cruise ship who see one another day after day but know that finally the ship will put into port and they will disembark and not see one another again.

The last conversation I ever had with the baker's son was in the last days of my last year in high school. All the Grade 12 boys had decided to spend a night together at the cabin of one of our number at Edwards Lake. It was, and I trust still is, a charming little lake surrounded by simple rustic log cabins that were used by the less fashionable families of Fernie, those who had not already staked their summer claim at Rosen or Tie Lakes.

The baker's son and I sat on the wharf, a small wooden tongue that lapped at the lake's edge. We dangled our feet in the still, cold, clear water — too cold on a June evening for a swim. Mostly I dabbled my feet on the surface. The sun was just setting and the last rays cast no warmth beyond the pink caught in the thin clouds that stretched like an old man's hair pulled against the deep blue of the mountain. It was like sitting on the edge of heaven. Perhaps it was the lighting, perhaps it was the memory of that evening when we were children, but I shared my dreams with the baker's son. By then my dreams were those of a man who wanted to conquer the world and live a large life. The baker's son said little, but he said words that have stuck like burrs to the edge of my being, all of my life. He spoke to me quietly and slowly as though contemplating each word to see if it was the right word to choose from the short supply he had left. He said, as he kicked at the water, causing its tranquil meniscus to break, "I am as happy as I ever will be. I could die tomorrow."

The odd thing, you see, is that he did die the next day. I won't tell you that entire story now, but it is enough to know that the very next morning on the way back from the lake there was a terrible automobile accident, and we were both passengers, and I lived and he died. I held him in my lap until the ambulance came. It carried us together to the Fernie hospital and I held his hand as he lay coughing up blood and something I thought to be bits of cauliflower, but which must have been lung. I sat with him as the last light left his eyes. They told me that he died shortly thereafter. I have never known if he realized I was with him at the end. I do not know if I was the right companion to usher him to Charon's boat. But I was the one who was there.

It was in the days immediately following her son's death that for the first time I grew to know the baker's wife. The custom in those days in Fernie was that people would often meet at the home of the dead during each of the days before the funeral. It was a number of days before the funeral of the boy would take place and each evening there was a gathering of his people. And then, as the family was Catholic, there was also the Rosary on the night before the Funeral Mass, there was the Funeral Mass, and then there was the wake.

I remember coming home after the accident, the blood of the boy still on my clothes and hands. I do not think I cried, but it is so long ago that I cannot recall for certain, although I still see the blood. I washed it off, over and over, as though Lady Macbeth rubbing the guilt from me. The guilt for having survived, and being happy about it, where the other had died. Unlike that lady, I do not remember the balance of that day, after the time, when I washed off the blood. I do recall the next day when the baker's wife called me on the telephone and asked if I would come to call that evening as was the custom. I wanted to demur, but acquiesced, though not without trepidation. I was a shy youth, and as I said, I did not know the baker or his wife except for buying and tasting their work in the sliced white bread, honey glazed donuts, Eccles cakes and apple and cherry turnovers that my mother sent me to buy.

So I went to see them, with the same apprehension, but grown bigger. I went to the little apartment just above the bakery that had been till the accident home to three. And thereafter would be home to two, until one day it would house only one, the baker's wife. The stairway up to the apartment was narrow and dark, and I think of Dickens, though it cannot have been so dim.

I did not know what I would encounter. I had until that time not often been in a stranger's dwelling. I knocked on the door and the baker's wife opened it to me. She greeted me. Her eyes shone, but not with laughter; they seemed to shine for me. I do not know what she felt on seeing me, but I imagine from the way that her eyes shone, and they glistened like the fresh blood that had been on my hands, that she saw even what I could not see. She saw what had happened to me. She brought me into the apartment and we went into the little sitting room. She introduced me to all who were present: a favourite aunt, eyes lined as though tears of red food colouring had been dribbled in place; a neighbour who wore her mourning like a mangy old fur coat wrapped loosely around her; the baker's son's cousin already a man who sucked at a beer bottle and looked like he should be somewhere else; and then finally the baker. The baker whose face was whiter than the flour that seemed permanently to be in his pores.

I quietly said, "I'm sorry." He looked at me at first as though I were a stranger on the street who had apologized for bumping in to him. Then, as he continued looking at me, I knew he did not see me. He saw only his son. His eyes did not blink and I could look deeply into them, and there was no colour and no tears, and I could see there was nothing left there. It was a look he would have for many years. A look that would never completely leave him until he went to join his son at the cemetery on the side of the slope of the mountain that cups our dead.

The baker's wife said in a kindly voice, "Would you like a snack?" She pointed at the table where an untouched tray of crackers sat along side white and yellow cheese that seemed to glisten with tears, as though it too were in mourning. Next to the cheese platter rested another plate covered with a few pieces of fruit and vegetables with a sauce that had not been dipped in. Then she spoke again, her words soothing: "Can I get you something to drink, would you like a coke?" I must have nodded for she left and returned to the room with a glass of the dark brown liquid, its froth settling from having been poured too warm.

The room was silent even though each of the other visitors sought to say something. Nor did the baker's wife say anything, so that I started to concentrate on the flies that seemed undecided as to whether the cheese on the plate or the sunlight on the little windows was more tempting. Yet she did not stop looking at me and her eyes seemed to speak to me and I believe they asked me if I was all right. And then all of a sudden as if awoken from a state of somnambulence she spoke clearly and her words were to thank me for doing what I had done for her son. But her eyes thanked me for being there with her son, for not leaving him alone, for staying with him as he died. She seemed to say, "This was no thing for a boy to do and I honour and thank you for it."

I could say nothing. I did not know what to say. There is nothing that a young man can say. A boy's life had ended, that was all. I had been there. The mountains, the sky, the trees, they were all indifferent, but the baker's wife, she cared about me. Each day, as I left the apartment that seemed to attract more and more neighbors and relatives, she would invite me to return on the morrow to join the circle of grief. There I witnessed an agony that was so intense it burned my eyes and caused my head to ache. Yet she was like a balm to the pain. And I took it, so that each day, I felt more like an imposter in that round, for I did not know how to feel the sorrow that they each felt; but I felt the balm. I do not know where my sorrow was, perhaps it was because I had not known the boy so well, perhaps it was because I had not yet lived enough to know how long death goes on. Their sorrow was in a place in the soul that I did not know. She must have felt my unease, for each time I came she joined me in silence and she looked at me and she gave me her hand and even her bosom and she made me feel like I was a part of this deepest place in their lives. The place where her son had been.

I carry with me from those days a vision of the Rosary as I knelt and complained to myself that my knees hurt against the hard kneeler board as we chanted the "Hail Mary's" and the rosary beads clicked. And I thought where is God in all this? I did not yet know the sacred beauty of the repeated incantation so I distracted myself by watching the baker's wife. Her face was wet with tears and I thought how her cheeks radiated light like the Madonna's who looked down at us from her place high on the altar. I thought how she was like that stone Mary who quietly and without complaint or recrimination sought solace in her God. I remember thinking, I hope she can forgive Him, and I wondered if I ever would.

The next day was the funeral. The pall bearers, each of us having been asked by her to perform this duty, met at the little apartment. She had solemnly conferred this task on us; entrusting us to carry her son's empty body in and out of the church and to the tomb. We sat huddled around the breakfast table, none of us sure of what to say to the other. We had the embarrassed faces of those who do not know where to look because wherever we looked we saw death. One of the pall bearers, Bill, a handsome youth I did not know well but who had always been friendly to me, offered me a shot of whiskey from his hip flask. I took it and it burned my throat so that for a moment I felt pain and it made me feel less self-conscious. The baker's wife did not say much to us as we shared her breakfast on that last morning before her son would be returned to the earth from which we all come. She looked at us and I felt then that she knew that if we could remember her son, some part of him would live beyond that day.

We walked with the baker and his wife to the church and I recall thinking how its sweeping Romanesque portal set into the tall tower where the bell rang was the appropriate place to launch a young man's journey into the afterlife. And the bell rang and rang. As I climbed the stair I stumbled and the baker's wife caught me so that I did not fall.

The death mass was, like all funeral services, both too long and too short. Too long because one must look into the face of death with no opportunity to look away. Too short because the final parting cannot go on long enough. The choir sang, the organ boomed, the priest droned and finally again the bells rang. We walked in procession down the aisle. First came the altar boys in robes of red and white holding crosses aloft. Then came the priest and I remember watching the hem of his robe as it gently swayed back and forth in rhythm to his gait. Behind me came the other pall bearers each with a face that had the beauty of youth marred with grief betraying how they would look when old. Then came the coffin on its platform with rollers pushed by the undertaker followed by the baker and his wife and all the congregation.

I can still see the vivid white of the hem of the priest as he went down the steps of the church and when I looked up we were standing at the hearse. The priest turned and looked at us and then he looked up the steps of the church and said. "I think you boys forgot someone." We looked into the portal and there on the threshold was the coffin sitting on its platform. My mortification and shame for our mistake was deep. I think the other boys felt it, too, as we walked back to the coffin and then lifted it up from the platform and carried it to the hearse. We dared not talk about our blunder as we drove the streets of Fernie up to the cemetery where we carried the coffin to the grave. As I stood there looking across the valley where the fresh green of June climbed the mountains that observed our tragedy with unfailing reserve, like old men who have seen it all, I wondered what the baker's son might have thought of us.

I did not have to wait long for an answer to my question. As we stepped away from the grave, where the diggers were already shoveling the earth on top of the handfuls we had scattered there, the baker's wife came to me. We walked arm in arm until we reached the car that would take her to the wake. She turned to me and looking at me with clear and untroubled eyes said, "You know my son is looking down at you now and laughing." And she laughed and then I laughed.

I never forget the absolution of that laugh and each day as I walk to my office on Main Street, past the old brick and stone buildings, I look around our village, and I see the beauty of the mountains that cradle us. I always marvel at their splendor. These beloved mountains which the baker's wife taught me, are not, all of them, made of stone.

HAIR

The barber's pole had a little electric engine which caused the red and white helical stripes confined in its glass cylinder to spin upward toward the infinity that is propped up by the mountains around Fernie. This motorized medieval beacon let all passersby know that here was a barber shop. More particularly, if one turned to read the sign painted onto the window in an arch of bold white letters, here was Putzi's Barber Shop.

Those who looked in or, if fancying a cut, entered, would see barbers in crisp white smocks standing next to red leather and polished chrome barber chairs, and at the back of the shop a sign on which was drawn a cartoon of a jaunty man with a broadly smiling face and a bow tie and smock holding scissors with the words, "Don't just get a hair cut – get'em all cut." Here the men of Fernie came to be coiffed, though they wouldn't have used that word. Rather it might have been a buzz cut or a crew cut or the classic cut, but most just asked for "the usual". Having cut the hair of the men since they were boys, the barbers knew precisely what was meant and cut accordingly.

Putzi's, beyond the sign and the chairs, was not highly ornamented. There were, of course, shelves with bottles of blue coloured potion in which were housed combs. There were some waiting chairs, covered in bland brown leatherette that did not seek to compete with the splendour of the throne on which the hair was cut. Next to the waiting chairs stood a little side table on which some back issues of the *Fernie Free Press* were stacked. The floor was black and white lino tiles for easy sweeping. It was a decor that made it clear that this was man's domain. No woman ever entered Putzi's except for a mother sheepishly bringing her young son for his first tearful haircut. Thereafter the boy would be sent on his own and the mother would return later to pay.

Putzi, Syl and the other barbers, and the men who visited them would have been offended if anyone dared to suggest that the main activity in the barbershop besides the shearing of hair was gossip. The men would have admitted to commenting on facts, exchanging the news, or telling stories or jokes. Some of the clientele who thought themselves more manly might tell some that were quite dirty or off colour. But they would have been indignant even brusque had they been accused of gossiping; as they would have been equally likely to assure you that this was what their women folk did.

The shop had large windows facing Main Street and a long series of mirrors ran along the wall to ensure that the barbers and those being shorn, as well as those about to be shorn, had as much a view of the street as of the hair being cut. Often the chat inside the shop was inspired by those who walked by the windows. If this were not enough fodder it also happened that the King Edward Hotel was kitty corner to the shop. The mirrors allowed the barbers and their patrons to observe the door to the hotel which diagonally faced the street corner. When the barbers were not looking at locks of hair, and the clients were not casting a critical, but discreet, glance at their heads, everyone was looking to see who entered and exited the hotel. Since this viewpoint was known to all the clientele of Putzi's it was certain that no illicit affair was ever conducted from the front door of the King Edward.

One cold and blustery morning at the beginning of winter when the sky was steel grey and snow had fallen and the weather was freezing Syl and Putzi were cutting hair as they had done for decades.

"Aw I don't believe it," said Syl. Even though he was a barber and should have known better Syl combed his thin strands of hair over the bald spot on his pate and then plastered them with a thin slicking of Brylcream.

"Believe it or not, I had it straight from Wally's mouth hisself, an' he was there," Bobbie said. He had grown up in the bush in logging trucks and liked his hair crew cut, not so much because he liked his hair short, but because he liked to visit the barber shop so that he could hear the talk.

"What's that you say?" Putzi was a big man, but his face was more like that of a mouse. He was sweet-tempered though he had eyes which darted about his shop in corvine curiosity and ears which stood forward straining for any bit of information that interested him.

"They was fishin' up the Bull." Bobbie referred to the Bull River, about a half day away from Fernie. It was a wild and tempestuous waterway that cut through crags in the mountains reachable only by the most difficult of logging roads.

"An' ol Billy got charged by a Grizzly sow. Not that it

couldn'a happened to a better man, miserable son'a'f'bitch that he is. The Grizzly rolled him aroun' a good bit before she took a bite or two. Luckily Wally finally had the sense to go to the pickup an' get his gun an' shoot it. Then he brung Billy in'ta the hospital. The doctors patched him up good says Wally, though he won't be out fishin' for a goodly time again."

"More'n' likely they shot sumpin' an' was guttin' it," said Lem, whose curly jet black hair was being cut by Putzi.

"Why'd you say that?" Syl looked over at Putzi's client.

"Nah, Wally'd a told me if that was the case. Nah they was fishin'. Specially with them new huntin' regulations," said Bobbie. Syl wondered if he'd winked, or if the man were simply brushing a bit of hair away with his hand.

"All the same, you know what I'm sayin'," said Lem who knew the ways of the bush.

The men nodded silent agreement.

The DJ on the tinny radio that Putzi had installed after the radio station had come to Fernie seemed to know that the conversation in the barbershop was stopped and so he announced the Swap n' Shop. "If you're looking to sell two pullets call 6008." Then the announcer chuckled, "What ever a pullet is." The DJ was a Cranbrook boy who wanted to make it big in radio and already realized there was no evidence more damning of Fernie than some of the odd things that showed up on Swap n' Shop.

"Complete dining room set for sale or swap for a truck load of dirt, call Elmer at 423-1119."

For the first time, beyond saying, "Mornin' boys," since he had entered the shop, Vernon, who had been sitting quietly in one of the brown leatherette chairs reading the *Free Press*, spoke. "Yous all see the mine's hiring more men." He chuckled, glad he was retired. "Yeah, they say they're bringing in a bunch a' Limey's." He paused as though to prepare them for the shock of what he would say next. "I even heard there might be some Paki's."

The men grunted. Then Syl said, "It wouldn't a happened in the old days." There was another grunt of general agreement.

The door opened and Syl looked over. Putzi slowly turned toward the door. Another customer entered. It was going to be a good day. With his ready smile, Putzi said, "Mornin' Tom."

"Mornin' boys."

"Have a seat. Syl'll be with you shortly," Putzi said pointing with his clippers towards the chairs. Tom, a short man known to all in town for sweeping the brewery floor when there had been a brewery and for a repetitive whistle which mimicked the downward trill of a chickadee, was one of Syl's regulars.

"There'll be more snow soon boys," Tom said. Tom felt he had special insight about the weather and always proffered his prognostication.

"Yep," agreed Lem.

The men's eyes, drawn to the door by Tom's arrival, stayed arrested there. Tom turned to look. A van painted with pastel pink, yellow and green flowers and a peace symbol in blue turned left and stopped in front of the King Edward Hotel. The passenger door opened and a young man stepped out. He looked athletic with a blond mass of curls that cascaded onto his shoulders. He opened the back of the van and removed a pair of long thin red coloured boards.

"Skis," said Lem.

Boots, poles and an army sack followed. The man placed the skis against the brick wall of the hotel, shouldered the army sack, walked up the stairs and entered the hotel. Another man got out of the van. He had scruffy bushy brown hair and a moustache. He was followed by a young woman with long straight blonde hair; the two stood pulling sweaters on over their t-shirts. Soon the first man came back out of the hotel, took the skis and poles, and once again disappeared into the hotel.

In the barber shop all the eyes remained fixed to the mirrors inspecting the van and the couple that stood in the street stretching and looking about. Syl was so intent on observing this event that the razor in his hand continued to cut Bobbie's hair even after the short lock had already fallen to the floor.

Lem said, "Sheeyt." And Bobbie snorted.

Putzi said, "Nothin' scissors and a dark back alley wouldn't fix."

The blond man was in the street again. He hugged the dark-haired man and then the woman good bye and they quickly jumped back into the van. The van drove away. The young man waved and turned back into the King Edward.

Syl didn't say anything about the youth. He just looked at the boy's hair, his finger's gripping the razor tightly as he imagined cutting the curls that swept in taunting smiles around the Botticelli face.

Syl hadn't told anyone that his own boy no longer let his hair be cut. His boy was a man and Syl knew he could do what he liked, but that didn't stop Syl from feeling like he had been betrayed. Every nerve ending in Syl's body trembled when he saw his son's shaggy dog doo. Syl's scissor fingers started twitching whenever he saw a man with hair over his ears or scruffy neck hair or bangs that hid his eyes. Syl's son had hair down to his shoulders. It covered his ears and fell into his eyes. The length of his son's hair was the only source of discontent in Syl's orderly life. It had gotten so disturbing that he could no longer sit at the same table as his son for any meal except Christmas dinner when Mrs. Syl, as she was known, could prevail upon her husband to hold his tongue about the mane of her dearest.

Syl's son justified his act of rebellion because he liked how the hair licked his face. He thought the way he pushed his bangs out of his eyes was sexy. It seemed that the girls liked it too. This was a further irritant to Syl because he fancied himself a ladies' man. His son was attractive to beautiful girls that no longer paid Syl any mind. If he had examined his anger he might have realized that it was not the length of his son's hair but the lack of his own hiar that enraged him. Or perhaps it was something else.

For a reason he could not explain, Syl felt this business about his son's hair had all started on the Tuesday before Lent in the previous year. Mrs. Syl had always observed the arrival of Lent by making a large stack of pancakes on Shrove Tuesday, or, as she called it, Pancake Day. Syl would arrive home in the evening and smell the pancakes with ambivalence. Syl loved pancakes, but he knew that a feast of pancakes in the evening meant that it was the last day he would be able to eat dessert for forty days. Mrs. Syl stopped making dessert for their supper during Lent. In their first year of marriage, when Syl had complained, she patted Syl's stomach and said, "I like a man with a belly, but forty days'll do you no harm." Thus, in honour of the Lenten Season, their evening supper or "tea" as Mrs. Syl liked to call it was completed without a sweet to cap the day. As Syl grew older this deprivation seemed to become harder to endure. Mrs. Syl was no longer beautiful and work and the tedium of life outside of work had reduced Syl's pleasures to few, amongst which the sweet with which he finished his evening meal and the wrestling or the hockey on television were highly ranked.

The Lenten loss of a few pounds was to Syl's mind not adequate recompense for the loss of his sweet. He noticed that his back ached more than usual, his feet seemed more swollen, and he was happier to sit down in front of the television. By the last week of Lent Syl was not only morose he became irritable and Mrs. Syl wondered if she ought not break the fast and serve her husband a dessert; though she was sure he was sneaking to the bakery every day for a donut any way. Syl might have been doing this, but a donut was not the same thing as his dessert, his reward for living through another day.

On the second Friday before the end of Lent there occurred a little skirmish between Syl and Syl's son. Mrs. Syl invited her son to supper and he gladly accepted. Mostly, when not eating at his mother's table, his meals consisted of tins he opened or the hamburgers and French Fries he got at the counter of the New Diamond Grill, which at first had seemed so good. After a while Syl's boy had to admit to his friends, "It don't taste like my Mum's cooking."

Syl's son arrived early and had already eaten some of his mother's pickles and fresh baked bread and butter as he sat waiting, his appetite primed for the full meal to be served. Syl walked in the door glowering because the corn on the little toe of his right foot had been smarting all afternoon. He harrumphed a hello as he went through the kitchen without looking about and went into the bathroom to wash up. Then he came back into the kitchen and sat down at the little arborite table where his son was already sitting. Mrs. Syl brought the cabbage soup along with the fresh bread to the table. Syl looked across the steaming broth at his boy and said, "Time for a haircut son." The hair on the young man's head was just beginning to tickle the curve at the top of his ears.

Syl's son looked at his father and then shrugged his shoulders.

Syl didn't quite understand the gesture, but it irritated him nonetheless. He felt he should have heard his son say, "Yes Dad." But his son looked at him as though he hadn't heard the order.

Syl said, "Why don't you come by the shop tomorrow an' Putzi'll cut your hair." He had never cut his boy's hair so that he couldn't be blamed by Mrs. Syl if the haircut was not to her liking.

Syl's son looked at Mrs. Syl, and said, "I gotta work tomorrow."

The three sat in silence, supping from the cabbage soup. Syl's son determined at that moment that he would eat at the New Diamond Grill for a few days. Mrs. Syl thought with pride that her son's job at the mine meant he would be able to afford a better house and car than she and Syl had.

Syl sat remembering how excited his son had been on the day of his first haircut. The father and son had walked to the barbershop together, Syl holding the boy's hand, shortening his stride so that his little son didn't have to run to keep up. Proudly his son had sat in the big red chair. Though he seemed a little frightened of the scissors and the shears, he kept a brave face. The boy had smiled when the cut was done and Syl had said, "You're a little man now." Putzi gave his son a sucker and Syl said, "Let's go to the Grill and we'll have a float," which they did. The whole time, as he recalled the episode, his son had gleefully beamed at him and Syl knew he would always love the boy.

The silence at the table was broken when Mrs. Syl started

to chat about the house that her son would buy one day. Mrs. Syl brought out canned cherries a concession to dessert and as soon as it was finished Syl's son left with a quiet, "Thanks Mom. Bye Dad."

Syl said, "Don't forget to go see Putzi."

Each day after that Syl waited for his son to come into the barbershop, but he did not come. On Good Friday the shop was closed and Syl started the morning with the hot cross buns his wife had made. Then he spent the day shoveling the remaining mounds of snow around his lawn so that it would melt more quickly. When this chore was done he had a nap. After waking from his nap he sat down to a supper of fish and chips which his wife had made in honour of the day and which he liked. Syl felt this was a good omen. He was sure his son would show up at the barbershop on the Saturday for a haircut. But Saturday came and went and Syl's son did not appear. On Easter Sunday Syl and Mrs. Syl went to the sunrise service and Easter breakfast. They sat next to Little Nettie Jackson and her misbehaving sons, which wouldn't have been so bad had the Fletchers not also been there with all their other grandchildren, too. Syl felt the Fletchers were an unruly bunch and it spoiled his sunrise breakfast to have a hullabaloo going on at the table. A man could not taste his bacon with the acoustics of the church basement amplifying the shrieks of the children as they ran about.

To make matters worse, Mrs. Syl invited not only her son to Easter lunch but she also invited her daughter who had married a car salesman. The two of them had already provided her and Syl with two grandchildren upon whom Syl doted. It was the car salesman Syl couldn't abide, but Mrs. Syl always wanted the family together at her table on feast days.

Mrs. Syl prepared a ham, frozen peas with her special cream sauce, and scalloped potatoes. For dessert she made Sherry Trifle. She and Syl pushed the chesterfield and Lazyboy against the living room wall and moved the kitchen table and chairs into their place. Syl put two leafs in to extend the table so that all the family could sit together. Mrs. Syl laid her only white table cloth over the table and put blue flowered plastic place mats at each setting to spare the cloth. Then she decorated the table with coloured and chocolate Easter eggs wrapped in red and blue and gold foil. To see her family seated around the beauty of the table was what pleased Mrs. Syl the most about Easter Sunday lunch.

All the family had gathered except for Syl's son. Mrs. Syl began to fret that he would be late. She had told him lunch would be served at noon, as Syl expected, and it was already close to twelve. The family sat down to the table and at one minute to twelve Syl's son walked in the door. His mother shooed him to the table and Syl said, "You're late boy." He paused. "Now for a few words for our Father in heaven so that we can eat." He bent his head and placed his hands together, "Father for what we are about to receive make us truly thankful." Then he glanced around the table. Syl stopped to look at his son and saw with his practiced eye that the hair on his son's head was a little bit longer than it had been two weeks before.

The family began to pass around the platters and bowls of food. Syl offered his son-in-law a beer which his son-in-law took and drank from the bottle. Syl did not offer his son a drink. Mrs. Syl noticed this. Saying nothing, she opened one of the brown stubby bottles she had set on the table and poured a glass of beer for her son.

The ham was passed and Mrs. Syl said, "C'mon children you all have to eat more, you don't want Grampa and me to eat it all do you? We'll get big like the porker this ham came from." She poked her ample stomach and the children laughed. She saw her husband give a little sour smile. Syl fancied himself a bit of a teaser and he liked to pull the legs of the little ones, sometimes quite literally. Often this set the children laughing in convulsions and giggles and starts so that Syl's daughter worried they might choke. She would say, "Oh dad be careful, don't hurt yourself." But this day Syl was quiet and he did not tease the children. Mrs. Syl and Syl's daughter began to cast sideways glances in his direction. When not holding his fork and knife he crossed his arms and either sat silently or said, "Please pass the peas."

Syl's son did not look at his father. He stuffed his mouth with big pieces of ham and he talked to his brother-in-law about the Lincoln Continental Town Car versus the Cadillac Fleetwood. His brother-in-law sold cars at the Ford dealership and was therefore partial to the Lincoln. Though both of them knew that it was unlikely that he would ever be able to buy either car Syl's son would say, "It don't hurt to dream a little bit."

After lunch the women cleared the dishes and the men pushed away from the table. The youngsters ran about the room, crawled over the sofa and bolted in and out of the kitchen. Syl's son-in-law said, "It's nice that Easter was so late this year, the kids not havin' to hunt in the snow."

Syl said to his son, "You didn't come by for your haircut."

"I was too busy Pops."

Syl disliked it when his son called him "Pops". He preferred Dad. Pops seemed lacking in respect and reminded him of those smart alecks in the fifties.

"I'm your dad."

Syl's son-in-law yelled at his children, "Slow down before someone gets hurt. And it ain't gonna be me." He fingered his belt. This irritated Syl who said, "They're not troubling us." Then, as though still speaking to his son-in-law, he said, "You better come in this week."

Syl's son sat quietly for a moment, then said, "I'm thinkin' of maybe growing my hair long Dad." He drew out and emphasized the word Dad so that Syl thought he heard a sheep bleating.

Syl's bland face turned white. His words came slow, the warmth bleached from them. "You ain't thinking of becoming a hippie are you."

"Dad, they even have long hair on Lawrence Welk, you don't gotta be a hippie to wear your hair a bit longer."

Syl looked away. He couldn't argue with that. The boys on the accordion maestro's show did seem to be wearing their hair longer. Even the older men on the show seemed to let the hair slip below their ears. But Syl didn't like it, not one little bit. A man was a man, and women wore long hair not men.

"You want'a come back in this house, you get a haircut boy."

"No Dad, I'm not gettin' my hair cut. I like it long."

"I'm tellin' you, you better get your hair cut. What'll all the men think, that you become a pansy?"

"I don't care what they think. Besides, there's a whole bunch a men at the mine that got long hair." Which was true, though they were sometimes ribbed about it by the older men.

"Well just hear me boy. You ain't coming under my roof until you get a haircut."

"Oh Syl," said Mrs. Syl coming into the room. She had heard the change in tone of her husband's voice in the kitchen. "Don't say that. Son you can come any time you want. I kind of like it when boys have a little bit longer hair."

"He ain't a boy, he's a man. And he should know better than setting a bad example for his niece and nephew like that."

"Oh Syl, come now."

"Woman, I don't want a hippie in my house."

Mrs. Syl knew that when he used the word "woman" for her he could not be reasoned with, at least not at that moment.

"Fine," said Syl's son. He stood up. His long legs pushed his chair away so that it hit the wall and he walked out of the house. With the determined footsteps, cadent arms and strutting jaw of a man who will not bend to his father's will; though he slammed the door like a spoiled child.

Bobbie yelped, "Jesus Syl." The razor's heat had come a little too close to the soft flesh at the back of the man's neck.

"Sorry." Syl's hand shook as he pulled the razor away.

The other men in the barber shop looked back out into the street. The blond youth with his cheeky curly locks walked down the steps of the King Edward Hotel. He walked out into the street. He stopped in the middle of the intersection. He looked down Victoria Avenue towards the high school. Then he spun back to look up the street towards the ski hill. The men in the barbershop heard a "Whoo Hee" as his arms thrust up in exaltation. Elsie Bingham drove by in her Ford Fairlane and honked on the horn. The kid just laughed and spun on his heel while Elsie slowly motored past shaking her head. The youth then walked to the sidewalk at the corner where Putzi's barbershop was. He sauntered up to the window and turned his face toward the men and smiled. Lifting his right hand up he made the peace sign. Then he walked away.

The men in the barber shop turned away from the window, and Putzi said, "Well I'll be." And Lem said, under his breath, "Goddam hippie. We oughta run'em outta town."

Syl sighed, looked out the shop window and wondered when he'd see his son again.

ACKNOWLEDGEMENTS

I would like to acknowledge: my husband who is an excellent arbiter of taste and has dealt with my artistic anxiety with serenity; my brother, my sister and my father for their support in both business and the business of life; my mother who has shed tears and laughed uproariously as my kind critic; my friend Peter Oliva and all at the Fernie Writers' Conference for their encouragement; and lastly Ron Smith for his kind and enthusiastic guidance.

Gordon Sombrowski began writing in secret at the age of eight when he wrote a six page story about Catherine the Great. Forty one years later his husband Kevin pushed him out of the writer's closet and into submitting a story; it was published. He has written numerous short stories, some of which are published as *What Echo Heard*. Gordon is working on his second novel, the first sits on his book shelf daring him to send it to a publisher. When not writing he helps guide his family's business and volunteers in the community with emphasis on the arts in Calgary, Alberta and Fernie, British Columbia.